# Sleeping WITH SASQUATCH

URBAN LEGEND EROTICA COLLECTION

# Sleeping WITH SASQUATCH

# HONEY CUMMINGS

4 Horsemen
Publications, Inc.

**4 Horsemen**
Publications, Inc.

Published By: 4 Horsemen Publications, Inc.

4 Horsemen Publications, Inc.
PO Box 417
Sylva, NC 28779
4horsemenpublications.com
info@4horsemenpublications.com

Cover & Typesetting by Valerie Willis

*Paperback ISBN-13: 978-1-64450-060-6*
*Audiobook ISBN-13: 978-1-64450-019-4*
*Ebook ISBN-13: 978-1-64450-017-0*

# DEDICATION

To Erika

Thank you for talking me into this insane idea!

XOXO

Honey Cummings

# TABLE OF CONTENTS

# Night with the Boys

**B**if's hair stood on end, signifying the time to shift drawing near. *Fucking new moon.* He gulped down his beer, glaring at the other men and women gathered around the campfire. Unlike his fellow shifters, he had a mop of golden locks and piercing blue eyes. Most of it hid under his ball cap, which only made his chiseled jaw and muscular neck and shoulders stand out. He shifted in the camp chair, and it creaked under the weight. Unlike the cozy office jobs his companions preferred, he'd spent the summer working odd jobs and hay bailing. His skin had turned a rich tawny color, as if the warmth of the sun had soaked into his flesh and stayed.

It wouldn't be long now before the change came over them all. Every new moon, they gathered here in the National Forest to walk the night as the notorious urban legends of the woods. They'd set camp and checked that no human had camped within a twenty-mile radius. Even the trail cams from hunters and researchers had been turned off, and any signs of tree stands checked and checked again. Being caught on camera caused a huge uproar in their secret community of shifters, whether a Sasquatch or a Chupacabra, it didn't bode well.

Twisting off another beer cap, Bif hated what came next. Everyone's cell phone alarms went off in unison and the ritual started. He watched with bitter disdain as the men and women around him started to shed their clothes. Bare skin glowed orange in the firelight and he was the only one celebrating alone. Again, Bif found the bottom of his beer and snorted. Seeing the smiles, the way hands glided to the more intimate parts freely and without obstruction only added to the misery he endured.

Last time he'd brought someone, one of his own kind, but she had broken up with him shortly before tonight. He thought it had gone well. They had screwed all night, and when the sun came up, they had one more round for good measure. He should have noticed after that the relationship was a bust. She hadn't been calling or texting. When they did talk, she was busy, but at last it came to a head three days ago when he caught her after work.

He could still hear her words stinging in his chest. *'I found someone else to spend the new moon with. Sorry, Bif. It's not you; it's me.'*

She had spun on her heel, giving him one more gulp of her perfume before sliding into a car. Not hers, but her new man's Dodge Charger, and it had roared away. In his mind, it had sounded more like laughter, and he wondered if she had used him for the last new moon.

"Bif, come on! Time to strip buddy! We can't have Big Foot running around in a wife beater and cargo shorts," Satch snorted, pulling his girlfriend closer to him.

His friend may have been just as tall but lacked the bulk of muscles Bif carried. He was just as attractive in his own way with his pompadour haircut and the deep brown eyes matching the bony structure of his thin face. Out of the group of friends,

Satch was the playboy, the one who always got whatever girl he set his mind and dick on. Granted, he wasn't afraid to use dirty methods to get that done, and Bif hated that part of Satch the Sasquatch.

"Oh leave him be. It was a bad break up," Abe chimed in as Bif shed his clothes and grabbed yet another beer. "Leave the poor guy alone."

Then there was Abe the Skunk Ape. His family had moved up north from Florida after most of their new moon go-to spots had been flattened for progressive projects like theme parks and apartments. Unlike a Big Foot or Sasquatch, his kind never got big. He wondered if it had to do with the swampy regions they originated from, needing to be agile to avoid the panthers and gators, but Abe always shrugged when Bif asked.

"Ya, leave this poor guy alone," Bif winked at Abe. "Plus, ya'll got some ladies to wait on. Don't waste any more time on the third…" He paused, counting the others. "Make that fifth wheel."

"Ya-ya." Kissing his girl, Satch started to stumble into the woods, tugging her along. "I told you that Bethany chick was bad news."

Heat rose in Bif's face, the site of the lovey-dovey couples combined with Satch's remark adding to his frustration. *If I had someone else, I wouldn't be alone. And it's not like there's plenty of shifters like us to choose from asshole.*

Bif cracked open another beer and shouted after him, "Does Yeti Spaghetti know you're banging his sister?"

"No, and don't ruin it, Bif!" the girl hissed, her petite body pale as snow in comparison to her dark black hair. "And I have a name!"

"Yea, I know it, Yvonne. Ghetti bitches about you every chance he gets." Bif raised an eyebrow but as he turned to his other comrades, they had all fled into the forest.

"Fine. More beer for me." He flopped back into the camp chair as midnight crested.

Ghetti the Yeti couldn't come out with them this time around. He was some place in Vancouver for a job, but that cooler weather during a new moon probably felt amazing. They called him 'Yeti Spaghetti' because he was more fur than man. Shifted, he looked larger than Bif, but the moment he went back to normal, he looked like a wet noodle. Bif chuckled to himself thinking back to the first time they met, and he had seen him shift. Shame he wasn't here to keep him company.

As the new moon crested, hair erupted across his body, and he groaned. Another beer, and he became more numb to the night and to the fact he was alone. Unlike some of his fellow shifters, he didn't grow bigger, just more hair or fur or whatever you wanted to call the fluff that came with the change. In human form, he was just a tall and overall huge man. He'd been labelled a body builder, Samoan, hell, even called a steroid junkie a few times.

Bif sat there, nothing more than a really drunk, miserable Big Foot. He'd spent plenty of new moons running the woods as an urban legend solo, but tonight, it hurt. Some part of him just hated getting a taste of something special, intimate even.

*If only I had a girl to spend these nights with... a girl who would let me make her happy...*

## Start Your Engines

"Come on, Frankie," Ted lugged the tent into the back of his old Ford Bronco, right beside the fifty-gallon tub of motion sensor cameras and recording equipment. Tall and built like a wrestler, there was no mistaking he was one of the good-ole-boys that made a girl wet just watching him work. Military haircut teamed with a long, brown beard ironically matched with a farmer's tan and hazel eyes. He could make any girl ache to spend a night with him. If that didn't tickle your fancy, the man had big arms and a sex drive that never ended. "We need to get out there and set up before dark."

"I thought you said we were going camping as a couple's retreat this weekend?" Frankie crossed her arms, bottom lip puffing out as she gave him a heated glare from under her locks of bleached-blonde hair. She had worn some homemade daisy dukes, complete with her bikini top and a shirt tied up so she could flash as much skin as she could for her man—for easy access too. Even with her thick thighs, wide hips, and big breasts, she still felt dwarfed next to Ted and his heap of muscles. Despite it, nothing could tame the brilliant blue in those eyes when she had a goal in mind. "Why are you packed like we're going out there to film a full production movie?"

"If we're going out there, I'm going to do some Sas-hunting." And there was Ted's biggest flaw. Whether it was the redneck in him or the nerd, he had a section of his garage looking like a conspiracy theorist's assassination chart, complete with maps, photos, and newspaper clippings all centered around the local forest legend, Sasquatch. "Frankie, baby… please, you know how much this means to me. I swear I'll make it up to you, Sweet Pea."

Twisting her lips further, she hated when he cooed her name like that. "Stop it. You look like a sad, lost puppy." Deep down her heart sank. Last time they were out together and someone mentioned Sasquatch, it had caught his attention hard. So hard that he lost interest in her completely. They had gone home early from the bar, and she fell asleep while he spent the entire night reviewing his Sasquatch notes because some new information had been shared. "This better not end up like the night we came home from the Nice'nSleazy."

"Frankie, Honey Bee." He came closer, his hand gliding across her abdomen, riding over her hip and grabbing her ass. It was aggressive and he pulled her against him. Oh, how she loved it rough, dirty, and the more domineering the man, the more she came. "You know I'm really going out there to have fun with you, Baby."

"Stop it with the sugary pet names." Her resolve waned as his beard tickled at her neck and he began kissing her, lips hot as they suckled with the threat of leaving a hickey. "Ted, don't. Last time I had to wear a scarf around my neck for over a week, dammit."

"Oh?" He nibbled her, his teeth grazing her skin and she crushed her neck close. He moved on to new grounds, suckling at her ear, sending chills across her skin. The heat of his hands crawled all over her, making her ache for more. *Who cares if we get carried away in the front yard? Let him bend me over and teach me a lesson for daring to give him a hard time with his nice hard...* "Don't worry. I have other places I can leave those."

She grinned, his free hand slipping under her shirt, snaking under the bikini. Fingers gripped her breast, squeezing until she moaned. "Ted, the neighbors might see us."

He laughed, twisting her nipple and his voice breathy in her ear. "Let's give them a show—right here, right now." Another twist made her squeal and she wiggled against him, his monstrous arm wrapping around her waist, keeping her from escaping him.

Frankie arched her back and Ted began kissing down her neck and across her collarbone. Oh how she loved the way his beard tickled her skin. Her fingers gripped his shirt into balls, and he slipped his knee between her thighs. She moaned and it only egged him on. Hot lips wrapped around her nipple and a silken tongue flicked it, each time sending a throb of want through her. Frankie closed her eyes tight, enjoying the overwhelming foreplay and secretly hoped the neighbor would be watching from between the blinds.

*Hope the crazy old bat has her binoculars!*

Catching her breath, she wanted to save this for when they were alone in the woods, but maybe that could be the encore. Nothing intrigued her more than the idea of losing herself to sexual pleasure in the wild, like the animal she craved to be from time to time.

*No, I want to tease him, make sure he'll forget all about Sasquatch by the time we get there.*

Pushing Ted off her, she spun out of reach playfully. "First, you give me that camping trip you promised, then maybe we can see about your little front yard fantasy." Her fingers caressed his groin before skipping off around the Bronco.

Ted licked his lips watching Frankie climb into his lifted Bronco, his shorts a little tighter at the thought of bending her over for all to see. Shaking loose from her tantalizing view, he finished tossing everything in the back. Leaning on the tail gate, his eyes scanned everything he had; there in those tubs were five wildlife trail motion detecting cameras, two remote feed video cameras, the camouflaged tent, cans of deer musk and scent cover, the laptop and pack of battery backups, folding table, camp chairs, and some MREs.

Smiling, Ted's thoughts said it all; *Good weekend to catch Sasquatch and a good fucking on camera.*

"We have everything?" Frankie leaned out the window and lifted an eyebrow. "Or are ya taking a piss back there?"

Snorting, he winked at her, closing the back up. Hopping in front of the wheel, Ted brought the Bronco to life with a roar.

# 3

## HANGOVER

The sunlight dappled down onto Bif's face, his pounding head making him groan. Before going for a run in the woods, he had downed three more beers and gotten bored. The whole night had become a blur before spinning and going black. He rolled over, but it didn't feel right. He felt stiff and bulky, as if he was still not back to his normal body. Blinking awake, he sat up, looking at his hands. They were still the hands of a turned Big Foot. Dread came crashing down on him. Scrambling to his feet, he inspected the rest of his body.

"Holy shit! This can't be happening!" The sun was up, but the shifted form never left.

Rushing through the woods, it took him a few miles to find the camp again. At least the sense of smell and natural navigation skills were something they all had in or out of the shift. Stumbling into the clearing, he froze. Knots twisted in his stomach to see only his tent remained.

*Did those assholes leave me here because I hadn't shifted back?*

After several minutes lost in thought, Bif shook his head trying to think what to do next.

"Didn't Satch go through this?" Breaking out of his drunken stupor, he dug through his pack and pulled out his cell phone. "I thought it was a load of bullshit, but here I am … stuck in a shift."

Pacing around the low burning fire, he took inventory of what they had left behind. At least his friends left him the essentials, all his things and a few other items. They were planning to come back eventually, but when? Scrolling through, he dialed Satch.

"Hey Drunk Ass!" Bif cringed, his hangover still haunting him. "Couldn't find you so we left."

"Fuck you for leaving me," he barked, anger seeping forward. "We both know you didn't even try hunting down my scent. But I've got bigger problems."

"You didn't step in a bear trap like Yeti?" Satch sounded a little concerned, his laughter ceasing. "Did you get it off? How'd you get to your phone at the camp?"

"I might've been shitfaced, but we cleared the traps before we started." Fighting the foggy sensation of his thoughts, Bif refocused. "I'm stuck in… well… I didn't change back. I take back ever making fun of that story and calling bullshit."

"No fucking way!" Satch started informing the other shifters in the car and everyone seemed to find it funny or scary. "I told you! That shit happened to me! It's no joke!"

"I KNOW!" He could hear his voice echo. *Great he has me on speaker phone.* "What in the hell did you do to shift back?"

"I had to go fuck someone … a few times."

"No, really, what did you do?" Bif rolled his eyes, looking for the clothes he had taken off last night. "This is rather awkward, Satch. I'd like to go home and do so as the normal me."

"Dude, I was stuck out in Yellowstone for a fucking month. I'm not joking. You'll need to find a hook-up. One round isn't enough so prepare yourself."

Picking his shorts off the ground, he shook them off. "You can't be serious. Hook up with someone looking like Big Foot. I'm royally screwed, Satch. Who camps out here in this shithole of a National Forest? There's nothing. Not even a good bird viewing trail! How in the hell did you change back?"

"Look, some hipster chicks high as a kite came and camped nearby. It was some naked spiritual thing in the woods. Far as I could tell, they were on one helluva acid trip and then some. Anyhow, there was a chick there... She didn't care who was banging her by the time a group of guys showed up, nor do I think she could care less about where she was. She just wanted a good time." Yvonne started shrieking, and Bif pulled the phone from his head for a moment. "I was desperate, Yvonne! You don't get it..."

"Shut the hell up, Yvonne!" Bif's voice roared through the car. "What happened after that?"

"Anyhow, I banged her and turned back. A few hours later, the shift reversed, and I had to circle back and hope they were still there." The car had fallen silent, the situation serious as the story unfolded. "It took about three tries, so... find a camper and give her the ride of her life. We all know you're the king of fucks. You got this, buddy!"

"You've got to be fucking kidding." Bif tugged on his shorts, frustrated at the whole idea. He didn't mind hooking up, but this far outclassed the level of two people intentionally looking for a one-night stand at the bar. "I'm in the middle of a forest. How about you all come back and help me or bring me back with you? Sure, I treat the ladies well, but c'mon, Satch! I'm a big hairy ape in this state! If a girl does magically appear in the woods, what are the chances she'll even let me near her?"

"Oh no. We can't take you home. It's a little hard to hide Big Foot in the car." Satch started to laugh. "Look, let me take everyone home, and I'll come back with someone willing to help out. Maybe post a Craigslist ad."

"How long will you take?" Looking around, the cooler had been left behind. "At least you left me with food and water. Beer would have been nice."

"I'll bring more and keep you supplied 'til you change back. Hang in there, Bif."

"Satch, I don't think I can pull this off…" The phone beeped.

Bif sat on the cooler, looking at the smoldering fire. His life might as well be ending. Worse, his only lifeline believed that sex solves all, and he couldn't be sure how accurate that solution would be.

*Is this what happens to a heartbroken Big Foot? Didn't this happen to crazy Uncle Lenny before he got shot by a hunter out here? Shit! That's right! Sasquatch Hunters tend to come out here ever since they caught Abe on camera. I'm royally fucked unless someone willing happens to show up. What are the chances of that? That Craigslist ad better work, Satch, or we may have to see if Ghetti's other sister is willing to put out.*

# 4

## Off Road

*T*he truck made a hum on the asphalt as they travelled. Off-road tires had a way of doing that and the country music didn't drown it out, but Frankie thought it seemed as if she couldn't have one without the other. She had slid to the center of the bench seat once they hit the two-lane road with the sign saying *Welcome to the National Forest.* It was nothing but nature and them for miles. No streetlights, barely a sign besides the numbered markers for the various clay-road off-shoots which led to more trees and reclusiveness.

Frankie kept creeping closer until her head rested on Ted's shoulder. He was wearing her favorite cologne, *Chrome,* and she couldn't help but still feel the heat of his hands on her. As her mind hungered for the lustful want, she began squirming in her seat. It wasn't the age-old twang of the *Nitty Gritty Band's Fishing in the Dark* that had added to the fire of desire. Even Ted shifted a lot, tugging at his pants to make room for the boys. Instead, when the low baritone notes from *Josh Turner's Your Man* began at the very moment the Bronco bounced down the last stretch of clay road, Frankie was feeling frisky. Her fingers slid over his thigh and squeezed. He tensed, grunting as he pulled her hand away.

"Baby, I've told you. You can't do that to me." He eyed her and she licked her lips before biting on them; she looked hungry, and he was on the menu. "Honey Bee, we can't. We'll crash."

"Stop the Bronco, then." She squeezed his thigh again and she could see his shorts tighten a little more. He couldn't say the idea didn't excite him, that he didn't want what she was offering him. "Come on, Teddy Bear. Let's have a little fun. You got my motor running and now I'm wanting more. Can't I play with you just a little?"

Her fingers snaked across his tightening shorts, both aching for more foreplay. He could feel her fingers through his cargo shorts, caressing his cock and balls and gripping them tight. Moans escaped his lips. She squeezed harder, stroking his dick through the fabric just enough to make him grow a little harder. Swallowing, Ted looked in his mirrors. No signs of anyone behind them, and no one had been seen in front for almost a solid hour. He let off the throttle, veering to the shoulder and without further ado, putting the Bronco into park.

Frankie licked her lips again in anticipation as Ted unbuttoned, unzipped, and flipped out his hardened length. Ted couldn't handle it anymore; he wanted what she was offering, and he wanted it now. He shifted in his seat and stretched his arms across the bench seat. It was all hers. The heat of Frankie's breath washed over his dick, and he moaned. Chills ran across his arms and his stomach tensed, aching to be in the wetness of her mouth. Silky and hot, Frankie's tongue glided from the base to the tip of his cock and circled there. He hummed, the sensation invigorating, and his hands fisted, fighting the urge to shove himself through her lips. The last thing he wanted was to skip this part. The way she played with him; the build that made the finish that much more satisfying.

Her lips were back at the base, suckling and kissing the underbelly as her fingers caressed his scrotum. The tip of her tongue tickled the flesh between the cushions of her lips as if she were French kissing his dick. Slow and in timed intervals, she worked her way up. Her breasts rubbed against his thigh, and he could feel her hard nipples. Each suckle closer to the top of his dick, only made him grow harder and Frankie smiled. She loved how Ted moaned, the humming of his pleasure in vocal form only made her wet with excitement. If he hadn't worn those work boots today, she could see his toes curl. It was pure torture for Ted when she started, and she wondered how long he would hold out before grabbing a fist full of her hair, aiming to finish.

*I've got him right where I want him...*

It had become a game, one where she knew she had the most control and it excited her. As she reached the top, she sucked the very tip, teasing him whether she would take him all the way in, her lips never passing the edge of the tip, but progressively daring to go farther. He moaned, his hips shifting, daring to cheat the game.

*Nope, not yet. I want you to know what kind of weekend I aim to give you, Ted.*

Pulling away, he grunted and frowned. She looked up to see his head tilted back, eyes closed tight. Snorting, she decided to change her method of attack. She began suckling and teasing the topside of his shaft as her thumb rubbed and caressed the underbelly. Again, a groan escaped Ted and the muscles in his thighs tightened. If she kept teasing, kept him wavering on the edge, he'd start to play with her as a means to encourage her to dive deeper and suck harder until her teeth nicked him.

*If you want more, you know what you need to do.*

Frankie wiggled a little closer, her pussy aching with want and her panties wet from the very idea she had Ted in a corner. His hand broke loose from the seat, riding the divot of her spine, slipping under her daisy dukes enough to force them off her ass. He squeezed her ass cheek, and she hummed against his dick. Ted grew harder, knowing full well if he wanted her to go further, deeper down on him, he would have to appease her needs. Another squeeze and another hum confirmed it. She would keep him teetering on the edge until he gave her a reason to go further.

*That's a good boy. Give me what I want.*

She scooted on the bench seat, positioning herself so Ted had full access to wherever he intended to play. Fingers caressed the folds of her pussy and she wiggled, enticing him to keep going. His fingers dove a little closer to just outside her vaginal opening, his fingers slick with her own anticipation. His cock pushed against her lips, he had gotten excited over the sensation, and she rewarded him for venturing that far. Her lips slid just past the cap and his fingers pushed inside her. They both moaned, wanting more. At once they dove deep together, lips wrapped tight around the base of his cock while his knuckles kept him from pushing any further inside her.

*Yes, yes, yes!*

There was something magical about the way he stroked her with his fingers in sync with the way she sucked and pulled on his cock. He was fucking her on both ends, feeling how wet she grew with his dick in her mouth and gushing as his fingers had their way with her. The tip of his cock hit the back of her throat and he moaned, losing his rhythm where he played. She sucked hard and pulled up and off with a pop. Ted moaned. Her tongue circled the tip and she wiggled her hips, hinting he would get nothing more until he continued pleasuring her.

*Don't stop now!* She suckled on the tip. *I'm not giving you any more until you play with me some more.*

Ted's agony peaked. His fingers dipped into her, hard and she returned the gesture with another round of deep throating.

He wanted to finish, he was riding on the edge of coming and he wanted nothing more than to have Frankie swallow. She was dripping wet, but she hadn't been moaning like he wanted. Fingers slid out and she pulled up and off his dick; the mirrored motion agonizing for them both. He grinned, his other hand grabbing a fist full of her hair.

*Oh, he's taking control. What will my punishment be?*

Looking down at her, both their faces red-cheeked from the heat of their toying. His finger moved up, circling her asshole, making it slick from where they had been.

*I've been bad enough to receive the full punishment for misbehaving, I see.*

Frankie grew excited, breaking her stare with Ted and began sucking on the tip in order to beg for what he hinted, what his fingers promised to do to her. She rocked against his finger, daring him to enter that forbidden place she yearned to be played with. His other fist tightened on her hair, and all at once, he dove his fingers into her; *two in the pink, one in the...* She moaned with a mouth full of cock, grinding against his hand. He was so stiff, every muscle in his body tight with the build of his oncoming orgasm.

*Please, a little longer...*

He lost it. Coming, he pushed her down, his cock riding deeper than before. Her tongue shifted and she began swallowing, and he released hard. He loved the way the back of her tongue and throat tightened over him, swallowing down everything he had to offer her. His finger rode deep inside her only pushing her further onto him and she gushed, thighs wet with her own arousal.

*Don't stop! I'm so close!*

Finished, he pulled her away, panting. Grabbing a work rag, he wiped his hand clean and shifted in the seat. Satisfied and winding down, he tucked himself away, and Frankie puffed out her lip. She had hoped he would keep going, to fuck her there in the Bronco and make it rock to and fro.

*I wanted to rock this bucket of rust until the Game Warden came to knock to see what wild animal he had locked inside until he saw my tits against the window.*

Her body hummed with the weight of her want. He had met his peak, but she was still teetering on the edge, just shy of the promised orgasm throbbing at her loins.

*Shit, I want to just ride this out a little longer... Fucking Ted.*

"Dammit woman, can you suck a cock!" He gave her a glance, seeing the disappointment on her face, nipples hard and thighs glistening. "Oh, Baby Doll, don't look at me like that."

"But I wasn't quite done, Teddy Bear." Breasts heaving, she wiped her mouth and frowned.

"You wore me out, woman." He put the Bronco back in drive and started down the road. "I'll make it up to you after we set up camp. You'll be walking funny before we head home, promise."

"Promise?" Frankie's shorts and bikini bottoms were sliding down her shins as she spread her thighs open. "Because I'm going to have to play with myself on the rest of the ride. Make you watch and hear me satisfy myself since you couldn't." The playful jab made him snort and rev the engine.

"You do that, Sweet Pea." He reached over and gripped her left breast and pinched her nipple. "And I'll lend a hand to get you there faster, Baby Doll."

Frankie moaned, her hands diving between her legs to finish what he had started. Her fingers were slick and the way they glided over her hard clit was intoxicating. She enjoyed playing with herself, whether he fucked her or not, she was never fully finished without the cherry on top. Masturbating right after a session with Ted always felt different, elated compared to those moments where she was trying to satisfy herself without the foreplay.

He twisted her nipple the other way, and she hummed again. "Let me hear you sing... That feel good? You like it when I twist 'em?" Back the other way and she moaned. "Don't make me get rough. You better come for me."

*Still, wanted your cock... but this... this might... this might do...*

She wiggled and shifted, legs jittering. Her face reddened with frustration. She was so close to an orgasm, and it was driving her crazy. Shuffling off her bottoms all the way, a bare foot propped up on the dash so she could dive deeper into herself. He squeezed her breast, massaging and flicking her nipple and she started to arch her back. He saw her bite her bottom lip and like clockwork, gave her nipple another hard twist.

*Yes! YES! Harder!*

It broke the levee. She lurched forward, a loud coo and groaning filling the air like a wave of relief and satisfaction exhaling from her. Frankie only made that sound when she peaked, and he loved watching her make herself come.

Catching her breath, Ted handed her the work rag. "It's clean, I swear. You're a hot, wet mess over there, Sugar Doll."

Huffing, she took it and wiped up her thighs and the seat. She hadn't expected to come so hard, but oh did it feel so good with his hand on her breast while she finished. Cleaned up, she shuffled her bottoms back on and slid back to the window on her side of the Bronco, watching the endless trees passing by was hypnotic as her eyelids grew heavy.

## 5

## Neighbors

**A** Bronco had roared dangerously close to Bif's camp, interrupting his plucking on the guitar. He snuck through the trees and underbrush, curious who his new neighbors might be. Peering into the clearing, he watched as a good-ole-boy stepped out. Bif cursed under his breath.

*Why couldn't it be a couple of Sorority girls on retreat?*

Opening up the back of the old Bronco, the man propped it open with a stick and began rifling through the back. Bif caught the extensive amount of trail cams and equipment. The man lugged out the military pack and there Bif saw it. The local Sasquatch hunter's patch. They weren't the brightest hunters, but in his current state of being a daytime Big Foot, this could be dangerous.

*Of course a hunter would come out and join me in my crisis. If I get desperate, he can knock me out of my misery or just capture it on camera. Good Lord, did he pack for a full production film or something? There's gotta be more trail cams in that pack than balls in a Walmart toy bin.*

A growl rolled out of Bif's chest and he couldn't stop it. Part of him was angry and the other part felt cornered. In this form, he was half animal and there were things he couldn't keep from happening. The idea of his rational thinking being overridden by instincts rattled him. Squatting down, he continued his glower at the man. Bif watched as he set up a table and laptop near a tent. Lifting an eyebrow, Bif couldn't deny the man knew how to setup camp and fast. He was curious why so many blankets for one person, until *she* came out of the Bronco.

*He brought his girl with him, but seeing how she's dressed, she ain't here for hunting.* The scent of her wafted on the air and he shuddered. *Peaches. My-my, she's horny and ready to go. She came all the way out here for some fucking, and I don't think he told her why he came out here.*

He could feel himself harden as he took in her perfumed fragrance. It was like ripe fruit, sweet and sugary. It made him hungry in a way he hadn't felt in some time since he spent the summer as a farmhand and hung out with a Chupacabra scouting for cowgirls. Bif cursed under his breath. She might be ready, but her sights were on her man and not the awkward hairy apelike creature hiding behind the trees like a creeper.

*How in the hell am I going to take advantage of this? I'm not like Satch, but...*

Bif scanned the camp and sniffed the air. There were no signs of drugs or drinking. In fact, strangely he didn't really smell food or any other necessities. Looking it over, he had set up for a weekend and packed for a day out. He glared at the Big Foot Hunter and what now looked like a disgruntled girlfriend, and he grinned. Unlike Satch, he'd rather have a girl clearheaded, and if things went south between these two, he could get on board with that.

*What fun is she if you can't tease her until she begs you for your cock? Poor thing probably thought he was going to be paying her all the attention the entire weekend. He's about to take this from presumed fuckfest into fuckup if he doesn't take it easy on the Sasquatch Hunter routine.*

"Ted, I thought this was about *us* this weekend." She frowned and Bif's eyebrows lifted high.

*Called it.*

"It is, it is!" Ted closed the back of the Bronco and Bif snorted. "Since you aren't gonna cover your scent, Frankie, just wait here, Honey Bee. Don't want your scent to scare 'em off."

*YOU'VE GOT TO BE FUCKING KIDDING ME! Did that moron just ask his half naked, ready-to-go-at-it girlfriend to cover her scent! That's fucked up. Hilarious, but not right. Poor thing, she really wanted to have fun with him, and she got...*

Bif's spying was short lived as Ted started to spray scent cover. It was pungent and Bif's eyes and nose stung. If that idiot thought it would hide him from one of his kind, he was sadly mistaken; though the scent of wanting from his girlfriend could draw him in far faster than doe in heat to a buck. It took every part of him not to walk out and give her what her body was demanding. Then again, Frankie's arousal had started to wane, and the smell of Ted's scent cover had brought both her and Bif to their knees.

*I'll have to come back when it gets dark and Captain Deer Piss leaves. He's ruined the moment for me and... Frankie.*

Unable to stand the scent, Bif marched back to his own camp. He had liked the feel of her name in his thoughts and wondered how a girl like her had ended up with a moron like that. Nothing in the Bronco or camp said he had packed to meet her needs. Well, besides the blankets, unless he was the type who didn't care to feel the ground under him. Back in camp, and far away from the stench, Bif grabbed his phone.

"Hey Bif! Don't tell me you're out of food already?" Satch prodded.

"Look, unlike you when this happened, I have a damn phone." Bif found the lack of urgency in his friend annoying. "And I'm in deep shit. It just got worse."

"Oh, c'mon now." Satch grunted over the receiver. "I'm posting the ad now, I swear! I think you can live for a while with a broken guitar string."

"Not that! There's a hunter camping next to me, Satch!"

There was silence.

"Is she hot?"

"Yes, I mean, he's not..." Bif covered his face, her scent still lingering in his nose despite the invasion of scent cover. "It's a hunter and his girlfriend."

"PERFECT!" Satch seemed too excited at the news. "I can delete the ad! You've got a solution to your problems. Good luck, Buddy!"

"Don't delete the ad," hissed Bif before a growl took over. "This is serious. There's not a drop of alcohol or drugs. This isn't like your little cult of naked hippie chicks. He's part of the local hunter's regime, but he's packing a crap load of cameras."

He could hear Satch typing on his keyboard. "I bet a hundred dollars he only sets up trail cams on one side of his camp. They're like a one-winged moth circling on a table. Couldn't find their way through the forest even if we put a yellow brick road down."

"That's not the point."

"Well, she's hot. And he's busy hunting." A squeak from a chair told Bif that Satch had no plans of bailing him out as he propped his feet on a desk. "Go over and say hi to your neighbor. Make a good first impression and the rest will take care of itself."

"Satch, this isn't fair. I'm in the form of Big Foot. It doesn't work that way!" He glanced in the direction of Ted's camp. "What do you suggest I do? You're way more morally compromised than me. I'm not good at being... well... a silver-tongued bastard who'd say anything for some pussy."

"Hey-hey." Satch sighed and after a pause, gave his friend advice. "Mistaken identity. It's gonna be your best bet and works like a charm most of the time. You act drunk and slide in the tent while she's asleep and do some hanky-panky and follow it up with the whole OOPS routine."

"I can't." Bif felt sick, he couldn't even picture doing it, let alone pulling something that dirty on anyone. "I just can't do that..."

"Look." Satch's voice lowered his voice, whispering. "It's not what you think you can and can't do. Morality is off the table, if I'm being honest, Bif. When I got stuck, instincts took over hard and there's nothing you can do when that kicks in and starts calling the shots. I wouldn't have dared to attempt the first time if it hadn't been for the..."

"Satch?" Yvonne's voice cut his words short.

"I gotta go man. Good luck." And the phone beeped.

"Son of a bitch." Bif shoved the phone back in his pocket.

The weight of it all crushing him, he turned back to the guitar by the wooden bench. He sat there, mind spiraling deeper as he plucked at the strings. There's only one way out, and he would have to find his own way to achieve the same results.

*What did he mean "when the instincts kick in"?*

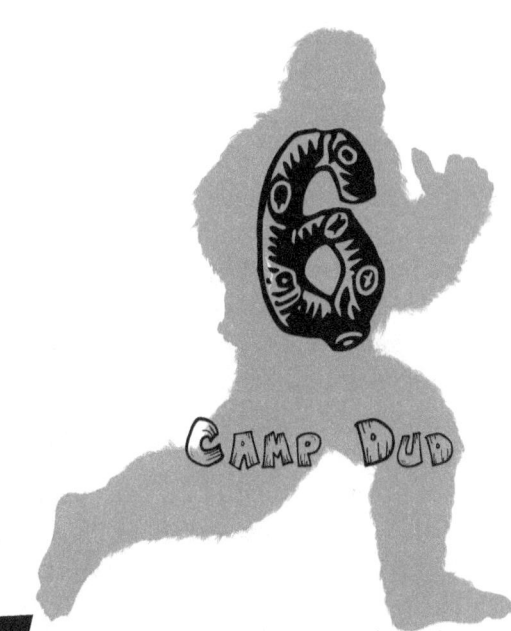

# 6

## CAMP DUD

**F**rankie woke to a loud skid and thud. The Bronco turned off, parked obscurely among some trees with just enough space from where the tent was set and the sun fading. The squeak and slam of the driver's side door made her stir, slow to wake up. She perked up, opening the door and stood, stretching her arms high. Walking to the back of the Bronco, Ted was taking stock of all the cameras he had brought for the trip. In a bookbag, he was loading trail cameras and more. She spun around, a portable table and laptop already set up for reviewing his footage beside the tent and she frowned.

*It's happening... I'm losing to Sasquatch already.*

If she didn't know better, he had a date with Sasquatch and not her. Spinning back to Ted, he grinned as he zipped the bag closed.

"Baby, are you planning to go on a hike or something?" Frankie watched as he slid the tub back into the Bronco and started to rifle through other supplies, grabbing a few bottles. "I just wore flip flops. I thought we would be setting up and just staying put. You know, you promised to fuck me till I walked funny?"

"I'm gonna set these cameras up and after that we'll have all the fun you want." He started to spray himself down with scent cover and the bottle after that made her gag and take a few steps back. There went the last of her sexual excitement and hope for a royal fucking this weekend. "Here, spray yourself down too."

"Oh hell no." Frankie crossed her arms and her brow lowered. "I hope you don't plan on being out in the woods all night playing Bigfoot Hunter."

"I prefer to call it Sasquatch, Baby." He was lugging the packed bag over his arms and his tone was serious. "It shouldn't take long to skirt the perimeter. The last time I was out here, I managed to record its call."

*Is this a joke? Am I on some candid camera show? What the…*

Frankie rolled her eyes, no words to possibly share with him at this point as her ire rose ever higher.

"All I got on camera were the sounds of him in this spot here. I think he's looking for a mate." Ted continued, unaware that she was disinterested and worse, pissed off. "So I'm hoping with double the cameras I might get a clear shot of a Sasquatch this time."

"Ted, I thought this was about *us* this weekend." She frowned.

"It is, it is!" He closed the back of the Bronco. "Since you aren't gonna cover your scent, Frankie, just wait here, Honey Bee. Don't want your scent to scare 'em off."

*YOU'VE GOT TO BE FUCKING KIDDING ME!*

"There's nothing exciting about that shit-smelling concoction that says we're going to be making love all night. Are you even going to be back before dark?" She motioned to the sky, tinged with the orange hue of the evening sunlight.

"I should be." He reached for a bottled water he had on the back bumper. "Get settled in, Baby Doll. Be ready when your

Teddy Bear makes it back." He moved forward to kiss her and she backstepped, the scent overwhelming. "I'll rinse it off when I get back."

Frankie took another glance at the campsite. "Are you going to start a fire before you go?"

"Oh no, we can't do that." Ted gave her a bewildered look. "They won't come within twenty miles of a campfire."

Frankie gaped at him. "How are we going to make food? Stay warm?"

"We got some meals, ready-to-eat." Her scowl didn't faze him as he continued. "And I brought some extra blankets, there in the tent. It's not going to get too cold tonight. Maybe when I get back, I'll share with you how a Sasquatch in heat sounds."

Frankie covered her face. "You'd better be back by dark and make up for all of this."

"I will baby, I swear." He glanced down at his cell phone. "I gotta go, Sweet Pea. Time's running out."

Ted bounded off through the underbrush, and Frankie stood in disbelief. She knew he had been obsessed, but this was downright ridiculous. There she stood, half naked, ready to get completely naked, and her lover... well he decided Big-Sasquatch-Urban-Legend-Thing was more important. Bored and disappointed, she meandered around. Ted had taken the keys to the Bronco with him, and his laptop was locked with a password.

*I can't even watch porn!*

Lord knows he assumed Sasquatches might hack his system at the rate he was going. She didn't bring anything. There wasn't supposed to be any down time besides sleeping and fireside meals. The ride here had been promising but snuffed out in record timing. Stifling a yawn, Frankie decided to just climb into the camouflage tent and start sleeping. What else was she to do?

***

A chill brought her from her sleep. She had tossed and turned, kicking the comforter off. Rolling onto her back, she saw it was dark out and an orchestra of bugs sang the praises of nightfall. Scrambling around, she found her cell phone: it was 9:30 PM. Rolling to her knees, she unzipped the door to the tent. It was so dark, she could barely see the Bronco, but it didn't deter her from slipping on her flip flops and coming out to see if Ted was back.

"Ted? Ted!"

Silence.

She texted him, but the phone binged: No Service Available.

"Son of a bitch..." Muttering, she looked out to the forest all around with no idea where to look or what to do. "TED!"

Silence.

*You fucking douchebag. It's been dark for over an hour, and you're still not back!*

Frustrated, her stomach growled. She was hungry and the only thing he'd brought were MRE's. She opened the top hatch and climbed up on the bumper. Hunched over the tailgate, she began digging around. Under her breath, she continued muttering her complaints about Ted, camping, and even Sasquatch. Her Daisy Dukes' button was digging into her as she tried her hardest to reach the MRE's. Even her outfit was starting to betray her, and she unbuttoned them and let them slide down her hips some and went back for the long reach, high-centered on the tailgate.

The top hatch had slowly descended and pinned her. She tried to push herself onto her tippy-toes, but all she managed to do was wiggle until her shorts fell to her ankles. She froze, groaning. *It's not like there's anyone out here with us...*

Placing palms flat on the bed, knees and thighs tight against the tail gate, she attempted to push herself out. The glass and aluminum top hatch refused to budge. Shrieking, she cursed Ted's name to hell and back before falling silent. *How long will I be stuck like this?* Despair washed over her, and she looked down through the dark at the MRE packages.

Squinting and trying to shift so the aching of her pinned hip would ease some, she opened the MRE, unable to read the label with her phone lost in her shorts that had fallen from the bumper to the ground. Taking a bite, she gagged. *Is this, is this supposed to be Chicken Fajita? What the...*

"Fuck this! Someone give me a Jack Link's beef jerky stick." She abandoned it, looking at the packs in horror, wondering if they were all the same flavor. "How the hell does Ted eat these?"

Shifting against the tailgate, she tried again and nothing. She had gotten herself at the wrong angle, her toes numb from the effort to keep them on the bumper. A chill rattled through her. Wearing a string bikini to go camping at night had turned into the worst idea ever, right next to thinking Ted could let go of Sasquatch hunting long enough to fuck her. She slammed her palms into the tub.

*I should have known when he packed this damn thing full of trail cams. I'm such a moron thinking I was going to have a weekend full of unfathomable sex! What am I thinking to come up with such wild expectations?*

# 7
## instincts

**T**he alarm on Bif's phone went off. Night had fallen and the short nap only made him feel more annoyed. He had stayed in his tent, waiting for Ted to stumble into his camp on his ventures of setting up cameras, but he never did. He smirked. Satch called it. Crawling out, he stretched and yawned. Crickets chirped and the trees were still, like black sentinels in the waning moon. He took in a lungful of air and tensed.

*Good gravy, I can smell her from here. Don't tell me homefry didn't come back and take care of business? This has got to be torture for the poor girl.*

His curiosity peaked. Making his way to the edge of their camp, he squatted so he could blend with the underbrush. There were no signs of Ted, and from the smell of it, he hadn't been in camp since he left hours ago. Bif began to stand up in order to creep up to the tent when he saw movement. He ducked back down and watched as Frankie scrambled out.

Her face said it all. She had gotten nowhere in her attempts to have fun with her man. If he had a guess, she hadn't seen him since the scent-cover ordeal either. No amends had been made, and now that the sun was down, it was his time to try and come up with a way to sweep her off her feet.

"Ted? Ted!" Frankie called out, but no one responded.

Bif watched as she brought out her cell phone. Most folks couldn't get service out here and from the scowl on her face, she wasn't happy to discover this. He could, but when you're a shifter who spends once a month in the middle of nowhere and never knows what trouble you might find, it helps to have service. The despair in her body language was hard to watch.

"Son of a bitch... TED!" Frankie screeched.

Silence. Bif couldn't chime in, not while in full Big Foot form. She'd go from pissed off to terrified and all hope to get himself back to normal would go out the window. Granted, he felt bad for her.

*What a fucking douchebag. Leaving a hot girl like that with no campfire either! And ready to go, just bust out your cock and get ready to fuck all night. Who passes that up?*

Scratching his jaw, Bif figured he might as well watch her and see if maybe a chance to sneak in and pull Satch's OOPS routine might help. Fighting back a yawn, he watched her lift the hatch and climb onto the bumper. She leaned over the tailgate, the daisy dukes and bright pink bikini bottoms drawing his eyes to them. He could feel himself get hard watching as her ass wiggled, bent over the tailgate. The glass hatch above her started to drop, breaking his stare.

*Wait, the stick... she forgot the stick!*

He stood up to rush forward, but the glass hatch had pinned her. Panicking, Bif ducked behind a tree.

*What the hell am I doing? If I get discovered, I can kiss my life goodbye.*

After a few moments of frantic wiggling, her legs dangled in defeat. She was stuck. Bif snuck closer, curious what she could be doing in there. She didn't call for Ted for long, but... the smell of a MRE filled the air, and he covered his face. Every moment he spent watching these two made it more obvious how shitty her situation had become. He started to reach for the hatch to free her when his instincts made him freeze.

*Oh hell, she smells like a hot peach cobbler, and all I want is a taste.*

He licked his lips, staring at her ass. A sexual hunger flooded him, and he abandoned his aim. If Ted wasn't going to give her a little TLC, maybe he could at least make this moment stuck in the Bronco a little sweeter.

*Just a little taste...*

"Fuck this! Someone give me a Jack Link's beef jerky stick." Her voice sent chills across him.

*Careful what you wish for, girlie.*

He could feel his throbbing erection tight against his pants. As much as he ached to feel his hard cock inside her wet heat, the smell of her had been intoxicating. Grabbing her hips, he would give her a reason to wiggle and scream. A cooing and purring rolled out of him, and he lost himself to her growing arousal.

*Peaches and cream...*

# 8

## TAILGATING

The heat of hands grabbing her ass cheeks made her tense.

"Ted?"

An odd chortle and coo responded.

"Are you pretending to be Sasquatch?"

*He did say he would share the mating call with me when he got back...*

Another chortle made her relax as the hands slid up to her hip. Fingers weaseled under the strings and her bikini bottoms fell away.

*Finally! Some fun! The reason why I came! Wait... were Ted's fingers always that long and fat?*

Frankie tried to shift to look over her shoulder, but the hands gripped her thighs and tilted her ass higher into the air. Before she could express her annoyance, a hot tongue licked over her clit and opening. A moan escaped her.

*That's what I want.*

Another pass, and she moaned louder, her toes curling. Lips started to suckle and kiss her, surrounding her clit and she couldn't keep her legs from shaking. In an instant, the pleaser had her panting and her body hot with want. Fingers dug into her thighs, fighting her desire to close them. With the Bronco hatch and tailgate making a barrier, neither of them was able to see or touch, other than the exposure of her ass and pussy. She wiggled and shrieked. The lips pulled harder on her clit and the tip of a tongue sent her legs jittering.

Reaching out, she pushed against the tub, her eyes rolling back. The night air invaded as he pulled away, chills rippling across her skin. Once more, the silken heat of a tongue travelled across her clit, licking her opening teasingly before venturing further. Fingers dove inside her, two digits thick and long as any dick could hope to be. She was so wet, they slid in and out with ease.

*Since when did Ted become so good at...*

Her breath caught in her throat. Fingers thrust ever faster, her legs shaking as she found herself coming. The stroking riding along the sweetest spot, not even she had realized how sensitive it could be at this angle. She gripped the edge of the container, her back arching as she came, gushing as the stroking continued. Shrieking, she lost herself. As her orgasm waned, the fingers left her, and she struggled to catch her breath.

Looking over her shoulder, she couldn't see where he had gone. Her legs felt numb as she wiggled, trying to get her feet on the bumper again.

"Dammit Ted! I'm stuck!"

*Where'd he go all of a sudden? He's got to be...*

"TED!"

"Good grief, Frankie!" The hatch lifted and Ted pulled her out of the back of the Bronco. His arms wrapped around her, a hand squeezing a breast and the other diving between her thighs. "Wet and ready!"

"Of course, I am!" His arms kept her trapped against the heat of his body.

Laughing, he bent her over, her hands catching on the bumper. At least her feet were on the ground and the sound of Ted's zipper brought sweet, sweet excitement.

*A fucking dick! About damn time!*

She wiggled her hips, anticipation building.

"Damn girl!" Ted's hands gripped her hips, making them ache. "You're hungry for dick!"

"Shut up and fuck me!" Frankie screeched over her shoulder.

Ted snorted. His hard cock pushed against her wet opening. She leaned back, wanting him to go in, to give her all of him. He pushed fast against her, entering his entire hardened length inside. She squealed, her back arching as a hand slapped against the Bronco hatch. Her eyes rolled back. She was still so swollen and sensitive from the first orgasm that she tightened around his cock. Fingers dug into her hip as he ground against her. Hard and deep, both moaning. Her breasts rocked and her face pressed against the tailgate.

Ted's hands moved off her hips, sliding under and gripping her breasts. He pulled her off the tailgate, her back arching into him. Ted sandwiched her between him and the Bronco. Frankie propped her knees on the bumper, straddling to let him grind deeper. Leaning back into him, she let her orgasm release. She could feel herself tighten around his cock. He squeezed her breasts tighter, moaning as he began peaking. Gripping her hands over his, she rocked, enjoying how he moaned over her shoulder.

Frankie began to squeal, and Ted covered her mouth. She bit his fingers, and he withdrew them.

"Dammit, Frankie," he grunted, finishing and leaning over her still. "You need to stop being so loud."

She shuffled him off, taking off her shirt to mop herself up. "There's no one else out here. What does it matter?"

"You'll spook Sasquatch." He tucked himself away, meandering toward the laptop. "Wonder if I caught anything on tape yet?"

"Are you kidding me?" Frankie tied her bikini bottoms then threw the damp shirt at him. "This was supposed to be our weekend!"

"Quiet down!" He punched in his password and began looking through trail cam feed of a billion bugs setting off the motion sensors. "It's not like I can fuck you non-stop, woman."

"Ugh, I'm going to sleep." Frankie marched past him and zipped herself into the tent.

*Why am I even dating someone this obsessed over a damn urban legend?*

# 9

## PEEPING BIF

Leaning against a tree in the shadows, Bif rubbed his cock. He wanted her bad, but he had snapped out of his lustful playing when the smell of deer piss and doe in heat came into the clearing. How in the hell Ted didn't see him or question the state of his girl was beyond him, but to watch and hear her? Oh, he wanted to see more, despite his better judgment.

He moaned, stroking himself. The flavor of her still sweet on his tongue.

"Dammit, Frankie. You need to stop being so loud," roared the half-baked Ted.

Bif didn't care for the rough tone or handling of Frankie, but he caught her name again. What a unique name, something he wouldn't forget easily.

"Shut up and fuck me!" Frankie screeched over her shoulder.

*I would gladly give it to you! Fuck Ted. He doesn't deserve a girl that hungry to make love to her man.*

Ted bent her over and the air filled with her scent. Bif panted, stroking as he watched them fuck.

*She wanted me, not him. That should've been me. I made her come long before your dick came...*

Grunting, Bif came as Frankie's shriek filled the air.

He caught his breath, wide-eyed.

*What the hell am I doing and saying?*

Bewildered by the hunger of lust, he went back to camp and sat on the bench. Grabbing up his phone, he called Satch.

"Hey, don't you know people are asleep at this hour?"

"Shut the fuck up." Bif still sounded breathless.

"Oh hell, did you get chased?"

"No." Bif inhaled deeply and freed it. "What did you mean by instincts? Like what kind of instincts?"

There was silence. He could hear Satch leaving his bed, the room possibly.

"Satch, I need to know. I'm not feeling like myself." His heart pounded in his chest. "I'm making mistakes and bad calls. I'm gonna get myself caught or killed."

"Look, just fuck someone. Get it out of your system."

"Seriously Satch?"

"I don't know how to describe it." He was whispering, something unusual for Satch. "I lost myself to pure hunger."

"What kind of hunger?" Knots formed in Bif's gut.

"I was ready to fuck any girl on the planet. The slightest hint of arousal on the wind smelled like... like..."

"Peaches."

"Yea, man. And it tastes as sweet as it smells."

"It does." Bif leaned on his thighs, holding his head.

"Oh, you got in there?"

"Not really, the hunter showed up and ended it."

Clearing his throat, Satch had one warning. "Careful. You're going to start feeling territorial over her. Enough you might have to bury her man six feet under. Fuck her and get the fuck out."

"Come get me," Bif pleaded.
"I can't."
The phone beeped.
"Fuck!"

# Good Morning, Wood

Frankie shivered. The early morning air, humid and cool against her skin was enough to stir her from her sleep. At some point, Teddy had given up checking his laptop and laid down next to her in the tangled nest of blankets. She scooted closer, cuddling under his arm and against his torso for warmth. He grunted, but his arm pulled her tighter, rubbing her shoulder to acknowledge her need for heat.

She had nearly dozed back off when he gripped her hand and led it away from its resting place, under the covers and to his morning wood. She snorted. After being ignored and rushed through the main event of intercourse, the last thing she wanted to see or touch was his dick. She tried to pull away, but again he led her back to his raging hard-on.

Half-hearted, she rubbed the length with her hand, hoping maybe Ted might doze back off and she could escape the unspoken demand. He wanted a blowjob, a morning one at that. Any time this had come about, she would be left unsatisfied, let alone played with. After the sub-par start to what she had hoped would be sex-camping, she had zero interest in pleasuring him. He still owed her, by a long shot.

"Come on, Baby," he mumbled. "Daddy wants a wake-up kiss."

She pecked him on the cheek, and he grunted.

"Lower."

"Teddy Bear, I'm not in the mood," she whined, her handjob falling apart and making him shift his hips.

"But I am," he whined back in the same tone.

"What do I get?" She pulled her hand away, making him crack an eye at her.

"What do you get?" he echoed, confused.

"Yeah, if I get you off, what's in it for me?" Frankie flustered. "Anytime I give you morning head, I get left wet and wanting."

"Aw, Baby Doll, I promise I'll take care of you later. Anything you want." He was tugging her hand down, practically shoving her face to his crotch. "I promise."

"Like what?" She pulled the covers back to reveal his throbbing erection.

"Anything you want me to do to you." Another push, he wanted this blowjob. "I'll lick your pussy all night if that's what you want."

"Yes. Especially after last night." Frankie's tongue circled the tip of his dick and he moaned.

"Yeah, Baby Doll. Fucking you against the Bronco was hot."

She rolled her eyes, sucking tender and slow on the tip of his cock.

*I meant that moment you were eating me out but, was it Ted?*

Before she could ask him the question and panic built in her mind, Ted grabbed a fistful off hair and shoved his cock all the way in. She choked and gagged, not ready for it this time. It didn't stop him from pulling himself in and out of her lips, moaning. He grew harder with each pass and as soon as Frankie could feel herself getting wet… he came.

She swallowed, a death glare on her face as she wiped her mouth on his shirt.

"Hey, don't do that," he grumbled, tucking himself away.

"Not like I have my own shirt to use," she shot back, rolling over and covering herself in the blankets.

"Oh yeah, well, I'll give you one of mine, Sweet Pea."

With a grunt, Ted rolled up on his heels and was out of the tent. Frankie squirmed under the covers, a shiver rolling through her in the absence of his body heat. After a minute, the tent opening blinded her with morning light and a shirt slammed into her face.

"Ted!" She peeled it off, thankful the shirt smelled clean and not sweaty.

"I gotta go check on my gear and want to look for tracks." Ted let go of the tent flap. "I'll be back soon. If you're hungry, there's MREs in the Bronco."

"They taste like shit, Ted." She popped her head through the neck of her shirt, and he was gone. "You've got to be fucking kidding me."

She zipped the tent closed and flopped back into the covers, wrapping herself up. As much as she wanted to go back to sleep, her mind wandered back to being stuck in the Bronco. Thoughts of the way the mouth and tongue worked her over and the stroking of fingers. Whoever had satisfied her last night, she wondered if there was a chance to meet them again. It was sneaky, dirty, but so was the fact Ted had lured her out her with empty promises while he played Sasquatch Hunter.

Rolling onto her back, her thighs wiggled. She was getting wet just thinking about it. Never had Ted or any of her exes given her the bliss of an orgasm from oral. Her fingers slid under her bikini bottoms and started circling her clit. They dove inside her, slick and wet, returning to the circling with heightened sensitivity. The way he'd suckled there and later the sensation of a tongue entering her like that. It had been so erotic and lustful. He had been hungry for her; knew how she was starved to be played with until she came.

She could feel her nipples harden, pulling on the shirt and making her moan. Another dive of her fingers, *so wet*. Again, a moan escaped her trembling lips. Her back arched as she circled, faster and aggressive, *yes!* She peaked, sucking in a gulp of air as her mind recalled the fingers entering and stroking her with such determination. As the peak rattled through her, Frankie felt a want and lust. She needed to find the mysterious forest lover. *Fuck chasing Ted!*

Panting for a minute, her stomach growled, and she frowned. MREs were not her breakfast of choice. Sliding on her flip flops, she at last exited the tent. Ted's laptop was gone along with most of the things he had left out last night. He clearly had no intentions in being back in time for lunch. *Bastard!*

The Bronco had been left unlocked, so she began digging around. As the sun rose, she flustered further in the rising heat and humidity. There were no more snacks in her purse and digging around in the glove box only resulted in typical paperwork for the Bronco and mechanic receipts. Looking into the back, her eyes fell on the wretched MREs, and her stomach turned.

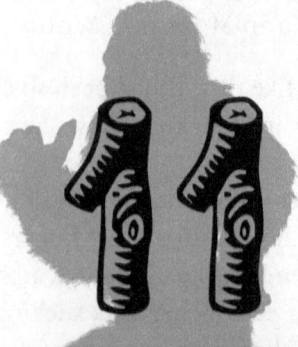

# SHE'S GETTING HUNGRY

**B**if couldn't help but come spy on the state of the camp. Instant regret slammed into him. They were both in the tent and from the sounds of his moaning, she was taking care of her man. Bif leaned against the tree, arms crossed. Anger and frustration boiled up inside him. Never in all his years had he felt so damn angry about... nothing.

*Why am I angry? It's not like he's fooling around with my girlfriend in that tent!*

Satch's warning echoed in his mind. Something had gone wrong in Yellowstone. He always glossed over it, never telling it in great detail, but he had been through this. Maybe he did find Bif in the woods and the moment he saw he hadn't reverted back, he packed up and got the hell out of Dodge. He knew the dangers and abandoned him because he was afraid.

A shudder rattled Bif's shoulders.

The tent flap opened, and the aroma of peaches made him tense. He watched as Ted, smiling with satisfaction came out to the Bronco and circled back. He smacked Frankie in the face with a shirt and Bif bit his bottom lip.

*Why in the hell is she dating this asshat?*

Ted let go of the tent flap. "I'll be back soon. If you're hungry, there's MREs in the Bronco."

"They taste like shit, Ted."

Frankie's golden locks mesmerized Bif. In the morning light, she captured his every want in a woman. Pulling the shirt on, her nipples pushing through her bikini made him lick his lips. His pants tightened, and he muttered to himself.

*Satch wasn't joking, I just feel hungry ... for her. And she's not even mine to have.*

Ted had vanished into the woods on the other side. More scent cover wafted over, and he turned away, heading back. The poor girl was starving. No fire, and no real food. He flipped open his cooler and smiled.

"Mama's bacon always did the trick; don't fail me now." He started gathering the supplies and the cast iron pan.

There was one bonus to the lifestyle he lived; he could cook like a pro chef on a single skillet with minimal supplies. Protein everything had been the staple for these things, so bacon and eggs it would be. Despite all of the smells, they did nothing to squash the scent of peaches in the air.

*I bet she's messing with herself. Asshat got what he wanted and ran out to play Big Foot Hunter. Frankie's in there just trying to salvage what she can and oh, how I hope I get the chance to do her right. Fuck you, Ted!*

He set the food in place on the bench. Scratching his jaw, he decided to leave a note. She had to have figured out that it wasn't her boy who had his way with her while stuck in the Bronco. He had been tender and soft with her, not the greedy harsh motions of Ted.

Happy with keeping it simple and short, he hid just out of sight. Plucking his guitar, he sang himself a song and waited. Never had he felt as much like a predator trapping his prey as he did in this moment. Frankie came into the clearing, and he stopped his plucking.

*How can a man resist a woman so curvy and beautiful?*

# 12

## FOREST LOWER

**S**lamming the Bronco door, she hoped Ted could hear it and cursed his name over it. Two steps toward the tent and her nose caught the scent of something.

*Is that ... bacon?*

Her head swiveled and she began to wander toward the smell. Her stomach grumbled.

*What the hell am I doing? Am I really desperate enough to invade another camp for food?*

She paused, the sound of singing hitting her ears. *Is that the radio or is there a man out here who can sing like Dierks Bentley?*

She took a few more steps toward the smell and sound. Blinking, she saw a tent and a table laid out with a grand breakfast. Her heart pounded, the music stopped abruptly, and she stumbled into the clearing. Her stomach growled and she looked around.

"Hello?" Stumbling toward the breakfast, she spun once more. "Anyone here?"

Frankie furrowed her brow and realized there hadn't been a radio, but on a far tree, an acoustic guitar had been left behind.

Her stomach growled once more, the bacon and eggs invading her nostrils. She turned to the table beside her and there she saw a note.

*Dear Bikini Bottom Girl,*

*Enjoy.*

*B.F.*

Frankie looked down to her bottom half. *Well, I think I'm the only moron who would camp like this, so they must be talking about me.* Her eyes widened. *Is this … Forest Lover's camp?*

Her tummy tightened. Uncertainty rolled through her mind as she looked around.

*I mean, clearly, he made breakfast for me…* She sat down, slow and unsure. *It would be rude not to eat it?*

"It's ok." A deep, sexy baritone voice made her jerk. "I made it for you, seeing that all *he* brought were those shitty MREs."

"Who are you?" Her eyes scanned the trees, but she couldn't pinpoint where the man stood.

"A lonely man wanting to make a girl's day." He chuckled, and her mind flashed back to last night.

"Last night, that was you?" She swallowed. A*m I out of my mind!*

"Sorry, I was…" His words faltered. "I've gotten myself in a situation and I started to take advantage… it wasn't right. Hope the breakfast makes up for it."

She could hear footsteps leaving and it startled her, "WAIT!"

The steps stopped.

"I… Look, I don't know who you are, but…" Frankie's face was red, the heat of the thoughts rolling in her mind both embarrassing and brash. She started again. "Look, Ted made a promise, and he hasn't kept it. We're done."

"Oh?" He couldn't hide the intrigue in his voice.

"But you…" She searched for a way to phrase it. "Last night, when you…"

Another chuckle came rolling out from the woods. "Don't tell me your man has never taken care of you like that, Darling?"

She puffed out her cheeks, the blushing never-ending.

"No need to blush."

She swiveled her head but still couldn't seem to find the sexy-voiced forest lover anywhere.

"I'll tell you what: if you need me to take care of you, just come back here."

"Ok, deal." Frankie's internal screaming couldn't decide if this was crazy or amazing luck.

"Now, you eat up. I promise you'll need that energy for later if you come back." And the steps crunched away before she could think of anything else to say.

Turning to the food, she picked up the fork and took a bite of the scrambled eggs. It was amazing. The man not only could show a girl a good time, but he had cooking skills. Picking up a slice of bacon, she hummed with delight. Not overly cooked and with the right amount of crisp. This was the camping experience she had imagined for her and Ted.

*Well, if Ted's not going to give it to me, at least Mr. Forest Lover was willing to do so!*

Frankie felt like a starved orphan, scarfing down the food until she cleaned the plate.

"Hungry, huh?" His voice made her blush.

"You have no idea." She leaned on the bench table, lost in thought. "I... thank you. Guess I look like an idiot, no food, no proper clothes..."

"Na, if you ask me, that boyfriend of yours needs to take better care of his girl."

It made her smile. "You play guitar?" she changed topics.

"Yes, ma'am."

"May I listen for a bit before I go back?"

"Anything you want, you just ask." He went back to plucking, the sound of it melting away her troubles.

*Dammit, this is what I imagined, this is what I wanted, and this is what I thought I had been promised.*

Frankie had lost track of how long she had been sitting there. He hadn't shown himself, but the music had lulled her to sleep almost. Standing suddenly, he stopped. The silence held strong until at last Frankie cleared her throat and spoke.

"I'm exhausted, but again, thank you for the food and the music."

There was a chuckle, "You're more than welcome to come back for more."

Her cheeks ached with her smile, "I like that. I might just do that."

Wanting to hide the heat in her face, she left the campsite in a rush.

*Dammit Frankie, you didn't ask him for his name!*

# 13

## TED'S CAMERAS

**B**if paced back and forth, pondering on his dilemma. His thoughts took inventory of the facts, one by one. He was a shifter stuck in Big Foot form and the only cure was to do the horizontal tango three times. Satch recommended sneaking in, but he had tried that. Between the animalistic lust and the idea of consent, it had left him in a wake of self-loathing. Granted, by some twist of fate, she was a gorgeous blonde and seemed rather calm about the incident.

*Shit, I must've done a number on her last night to forgive me so easily. She even got a little turned on thinking about it.*

A smile bloomed on his face, and he couldn't let it go. If he played his cards right, he might end up with a new girlfriend at this rate, or at least the best damn weekend hookup ever. The main obstacle was her man, Ted the Sasquatch Hunter. Looking around, he grabbed up his ball cap and with a groan, pulled on his hoodie. He looked like a gorilla in a skater punk outfit, but it would at least obscure the fact he was indeed Big Foot.

He skirted the outside of Frankie and Ted's campsite. He could tell she was asleep in the tent, and he sat on a laptop reviewing trail cam feed. Spitting at the ground, Bif made his way around and started taking inventory of all the equipment on the trees.

*Good grief, a deer hunter has more sense than this.*

He tapped a trail cam with his foot, and it fell off the tree. Chuckling, he squatted down and pulled the SD card out and snapped it in half. Ted had run the plastic tie strips the wrong way and with just the slightest tug, the cams were coming loose.

Despite that, he had to be more leery of the wireless cameras he'd drilled into the side of the pine trees and firs. Granted, they gave themselves away with long lines of sap dripping down the side of the tree. Laughing again, he tilted them up and shook his head that the man didn't even try to paint the white casing black or green.

*Is he a rookie at this? Hoping to return half this shit to Walmart when they get back?*

Mapping out the cameras didn't take long either. Like Satch had suggested, Ted had managed to make a singular circle on the north side of his camp. Satisfied he'd disrupted most of the cameras, Bif started to back track to their camp to see what else he could sabotage just in case. Footsteps and broken branches littered the area. This hunter had been beyond sloppy.

*You failed to please your girl in hopes of catching me on camera. Looking at your attempt at that, you're failing at that too, Captain Deer Piss.*

Bif snorted to himself as he sauntered along.

"I think I found a print!" Ted's voice shot through Bif, and he stopped.

*Where? My camp?*

Eyes wide in alarm, he snuck closer as the couple began to argue. Bif dared to get close, real close, and there he saw Ted's sticks and bright caution tape.

*Shit! Behind the Bronco!*

"NOT LIKE THIS, TED!" Frankie's voice brought Bif's eyes up in time to see her burst out of the tent. "We're done."

*And that means she's all mine to have. Good luck hunting with broken cams, Ted!*

Heart pounding, Bif rushed back to his camp. Grinning like a fool, he shed his hoodie and sat hidden in the shade. He could still hear them arguing. There weren't many choices as to where Frankie could go, and after this morning and last night's interlude, he hoped she'd come his way.

Looking down at this guitar, he picked it up and started playing. At least he could pass the time and hide his excitement this way. Something about playing kept the animalistic lust at bay, but he wanted to take her, claim her as his.

*If she's done with the hunter, then it's time to show her the animal.*

# 14

## Lunch Goes Long

Ted woke Frankie with a nudge of his boot, and she rolled to face him, frowning.

"You gonna sleep the day away?" He lifted an eyebrow.

"Well, I was hoping to fuck the day away, but you've been gone for most of this camping trip." She rolled back over. "How's the hunting going?"

"I think I found a print!" His excitement was ill-timed.

"Oh goodie." Frankie rolled her eyes, stifling a yawn.

"I need to check the trail cams," he announced, unpacking the laptop and various cameras and SD cards at the table. "It was close to one, maybe I caught Sasquatch on camera finally."

"Ted, this was supposed to be *our time together*." She sat up, glaring into his back through the tent opening.

"It is, Sweet Pea." He didn't even turn to talk to her.

"No, it's not. You're busy smelling like deer piss and hunting an urban legend."

"I thought you'd want to join me."

"NOT LIKE THIS, TED!" She burst out of the tent, her frustration peaking. "We're done."

54

"Wait, what?" He finally met her gaze as she towered over him, arms crossed. "Done?"

"It's over. This trip, this relationship, and us. DONE." She growled. "Over. Take me home."

His brow furrowed. "I'll take you home when I'm ready to leave."

"And when will that be?" she hissed.

"Tomorrow." He slammed the laptop closed and started packing up his stuff. "Since I don't have to worry about taking care of you, I'll go back to hunting."

"What? Are you kidding me!" He was marching out to the woods. "Dammit, Ted!"

She let him go, the scent cover and animal piss making her stomach turn.

Turning to the Bronco, she pulled out her cell phone. No signal. Letting out a frustrated scream, she looked around the camp. This was supposed to be the ultimate date weekend. Instead, she had been roped into it so he could run off into the woods but still get his share of blowjobs. Looking at everything, the image of him marching off, it hit her. He never intended to give her a minute of his time. The asshole had packed for a full production hunt and not one plan to get kinky with her in the wild. He figured she'd be a puppy dog that would sit and wait like a good girl for him.

"Fuck you, Ted!"

Looking at the time on her phone, it was pushing a little after noon. She looked down at her bare legs and bikini bottoms with disdain. She felt stupid. Naïve. And all she wanted was someone to love her physically and emotionally. Ted had proven he had aimed to have his needs cared for and had abandoned hers.

Silence fell on the forest and like a whisper on the wind, she could hear the plucking of a guitar and the humming of a baritone voice. *Forest lover... should I take a chance on a stranger?* She looked up at the dappled sky through the tree branches. *What do I have to lose? It'll make one hell of a story to share, I suppose.* She grinned. *I wanted a weekend of fucking, and I'm going to make that happen!*

Frankie marched toward Forest Lover's camp. Before she got close, his singing and playing had ceased. It made her freeze.

"You came back sooner than I thought." He spoke through the wall of trees and underbrush.

"Well, we got into a fight," she blurted.

"I heard it from here."

"Sorry..." She continued into the clearing and once more found herself alone, the guitar leaning on a tree. "Am I not allowed to see you or something?"

"Well, about that..." He seemed nervous. "It's about my situation. It may be best to not see me just yet."

"Are you horribly scarred or something?" Her face flushed. "I mean, not that it matters..."

"Scarred." He echoed as if calculating the meaning of the word. "I suppose we can call it that."

"So..." She tugged on the hem of her shirt, looking down at her feet.

Her eyes widened. One foot had landed within a bare-footed print and not one part of her flip flop touched the edges.

*Damn, he's got a big foot! What is that, size fourteen? Bigger?* She smirked, a thought from her teen years creeping forward. *You know what they say about a man with large feet...*

"Did you get hungry again?" His voice cut through her thoughts.

"N-no... well... in some way." Her determination and bravery crept forward. She had made up her mind before marching here so it was time to make the offer known.

"Hungry in what way?" The tone made it clear he had some inkling of what she came to offer him.

"Well, shit, I'm trying to ask this without sounding like a complete whore, but…" Closing her eyes, she puffed out her cheeks a moment before balling her hands into fists. "I came out here to fuck and if Ted won't deliver, I figured maybe you'd be interested."

Silence filled the air and her stomach knotted.

*Was that too forward? I mean, isn't it every man's dream to be made an offer by some hot blonde in a bikini to fuck his brain's out on a whim while out camping? Good grief, this sounds like a bad porno film…*

"I'm sorry…. I'll just leave…" Frankie spun on her heel, feeling like an utter fool.

"Wait." There it was; the bark of a baritone that made her weak in the knees. "Close your eyes."

"What?" She twisted around toward the sound of his voice but still couldn't see him anywhere.

"Promise me you'll keep your eyes closed until I tell you it's okay." His tone was deep and steady. He was serious.

"First, tell me your name." Frankie lifted her chin. *At least get the man's name beforehand, good gracious!* "I'm Frankie."

"I heard your name from your … now ex." He scoffed, and with a sigh she could hear from where she stood, he let his name fly. "You can call me Bif."

"Bif," she echoed, trying out the name. "Ok, Bif. I'll close my eyes, but I can't promise during the deed if they'll stay that way."

"R-right." He hadn't thought of that, and she heard him rifling around. "I have a bandana. Will it be okay if I blindfold you? Just in case."

*Kinky.* Closing her eyes tight, Frankie threw her arms out. "Come blindfold me then! Eyes are shut tight. Promise!"

Footsteps came closer and Frankie swallowed. Excitement and fear tangled together as he circled her like a predator. A finger caressed across her arm, goosebumps rippling across her skin. As the finger rode over her shoulder, she could feel the heat of his body behind her. *Ted has nothing on this man!* He tucked her hair behind her ear. A shiver rattled her shoulders as the heat of his breath washed over her neck.

"I'm going to blindfold you now, Frankie." His baritone voice rumbled into her ear, and she ached for him. "I promise I'll make sure you'll enjoy every minute of this."

"Promise?" He tied the blindfold tight and Frankie bit her bottom lip.

"Let me know if I kept it after we're done," he teased, his lips kissing her neck.

Hands, large and making Frankie feel small, cupped her shoulders. They encouraged her arms to fall, to relax. She let herself lean back into him, his hard-on making her gasp. *Will that even fit! He's built like a horse!* His arms wrapped around her, pulling her tighter against him. He suckled at her neck, and she tilted her head to let him have more access. Thoughts of the Bronco last night flashed into her mind and her body heated at the memory.

A hand glided across the skin of her stomach, sliding under her shirt and bikini to cup her breast. She hummed as he kneaded her flesh and began kissing down and across her shoulder. The other hand found the top of her hip and snuck under her bottoms. Fingers dove between her thighs, finding her clit with precision and she jerked. The touch of him was electrifying and he giggled at her shudder.

"You okay?" he whispered into her ear.

She wiggled against him, the muscles in his arms hardening to keep her in place as his fingers worked.

"I... I can't help it," she breathed as her hands gripped at his arms.

His hard cock rubbed against her lower backside, and she could feel herself getting wet with anticipation. "I've barely gotten started and you're already..." Fingers teased, daring to dip inside her, and came back slick as they circled her clit.

Her breath caught. A jolt made her stiffen before her knees started to go weak. Something about his touch was like nothing she had experienced before. Her breath quickened with the rise of her heartbeat. With each circle, she let herself fall further into the bulk of his body. The sensation of his breath on her neck as he nuzzled her only added to the shivers racking her body from head to toe.

*I'm going to die; this feels too good...*

"Girl, you're falling down on me," he breathed, groaning as his cock throbbed sandwiched between their bodies. "Where you want to do this? I'll carry you anywhere you want."

Frankie tried to open her eyes, but the bandana obscured her view. The image of the wooden bench she had eaten at this morning flashed in her mind and she bit her lip. *Should I dare to make such a bold request? Fucking me out in the open, where Ted just might hear us, no... see us.* She grew a little wetter, her loins throbbing. *Fuck Ted! Let him see and hear what he could have had!*

"The bench," she whispered, unsure how Bif might take it.

Without another word, he spun her around and lifted her up by her ass cheeks. She straddled him, thighs on his hip and a monstrous erection under his pants rubbing against her... she moaned, aching to see what a big dick like that might feel like. He sat her on top of the bench, her feet on the bench seat as he pulled away from her. Hands free, Frankie wasted no time abandoning Ted's shirt and began pulling the strings of her top. She could feel Bif pulling the strings and unknotting her bottoms.

"Scoot further onto the edge," he breathed before the heat of his lips wrapped around her nipple. Arching her back, she shifted to where he needed her to be. She moaned, the heat of his hands sliding up her legs, shifting to finish their journey along her inner thighs. A thumb rode across her wet pussy and continued the work he had abandoned. She jerked forward, legs failing to close as her knees locked against large shoulders.

*So much bigger than Ted... so big...*

Blindly, she reached forward but his hand caught both her wrists. "No touching me just yet. Let me enjoy you a little longer. You'll need these in a minute..." He let go.

*How scarred is the poor man? Screw it, the man is an amazing lover, and I haven't made it to the main course yet!*

She rested her palms behind her, widening her legs. If he wanted to enjoy her, then she would open herself up and let him have all he could handle. The thumb began circling again and her legs shook. The other hand glided against her inner thigh and two fingers slid inside her. She groaned. He was slow and deliberate, pulling them all the way out before descending slowly back into her depths. She tightened on his fingers, and he seemed to growl in response.

*I wanted wild hot sex in the forest ... and that's what's finally happening. Oh, but please, I can't stand this...*

Frankie wiggled, grinding against his hand and knuckles on the third entry. "Faster."

"No. I'm still playing..." his voice obscured by a growl.

"Please..." she wiggled, impatient. *Surely having a hard-on for this long has to be driving him wild. Ted can't go a full fifteen minutes without shoving in me or in my mouth.*

The hands pulled away and she whimpered. Before she could say another word, his hands pushed her legs wide and the silken heat of his tongue sent a shocking wave of euphoria over her. She lurched forward. Fleshy lips suckled on her clit, and she teetered on the edge of an orgasm. Her shaking legs squeezed around his shoulders, and she arched her back, shrieking.

Fingers teased her with the threat of coming back inside her, the tips just passed the threshold, agonizing and exciting. She flustered, never had she felt so damn wet. Shifting her hips, she wanted more. His teeth threatened her clit, and she shrieked as he thrust his fingers in and out with uncanny speed. She folded on top of him, fingers gripping the hair on top of his head. She came, hard and wet. It was the first time she had ever felt the rush of fluids in response to being toyed with so heavily.

Panting, her body shook from the orgasm, but was given no relief from the breathtaking pleasure. His lips left her clit with a pop of suction, earning another squeal. A deep inhale and the heat of a tongue gliding inside her sent her arching, releasing his hair to catch herself. She let herself lay across the wooden bench. A hand glided up her thigh, across her hip and abdomen before finding a bare breast. He caught her nipple between a finger and thumb, and she squirmed.

His tongue flicked her clit, and he sucked it once more. Fingers moved in and out again and before she could voice how overwhelmed with arousal she was, she came again. Breathless, he pulled away and she was quick to shut her legs, her inner thighs hot, wet, and throbbing. Frankie hummed as she rode out the second wave of delight. But she wanted more, wanted him, wanted that throbbing erection she had felt at the start of this inside her.

"I want you…" she huffed, cursing the bandana. "I want you inside me."

The sound of a zipper and pants dropping made her throbbing grow. "Open your legs and let me in."

Panting, she fought against her body and parted her thighs. The heat of his body slipped between them, and the tip of his hard cock rubbed against her opening.

"Are you sure?" His voice was husky and breathless with his own desire to be inside her. "If I'm too big…"

"Fuck me…" she blurted, crazed with want. "I'm wet for you, now fuck me."

At first, he was slow, her wetness making him glide in with ease. He moaned as he entered her. She ached and relaxed and tightened and at last her breath caught. Never had she felt so filled by a man. Hip against hip, he paused. He leaned down, suckling one breast then the other. Frankie's hands had found the edges of the bench and gripped them. White-knuckled, she started the grind, adjusting and loving how big he felt inside her. Every little motion made him throb and it sent waves through her, and she wanted more. The suckling of her nipples had excited him, the shift of her hip had made him throb, and now he started to stroke in and out, slowly.

Each time he slid back inside, her breath caught, and he would pause. She would tighten and loosen, and they repeated this teasing and cautious moment a few times. Frankie wanted to feel how big he was, and one hand slid between them. Both moaned; Bif throbbed, and Frankie moaned as her hand failed to complete the grip. The motion pushed him to speed up, both moaning as she grew wet with each stroke and his throbbing cock slid faster.

Her back arched, an orgasm beginning to peak. He leaned down sucking her breast and teasing her nipple with his teeth. She began to shriek as his growling pushed it over the tipping point. He began moaning and pushed hard against her as he came with her.

"Oh!" Frankie's shrill scream caught in her breath.

His throbbing erection sent her into a second orgasm. The hardness of his erection as he came only amplified everything that had become so sensual in the course of what had happened.

Bif slid the bandana off, and she squinted up at him through the wave of ecstasy.

*My God, he's fucking gorgeous!*

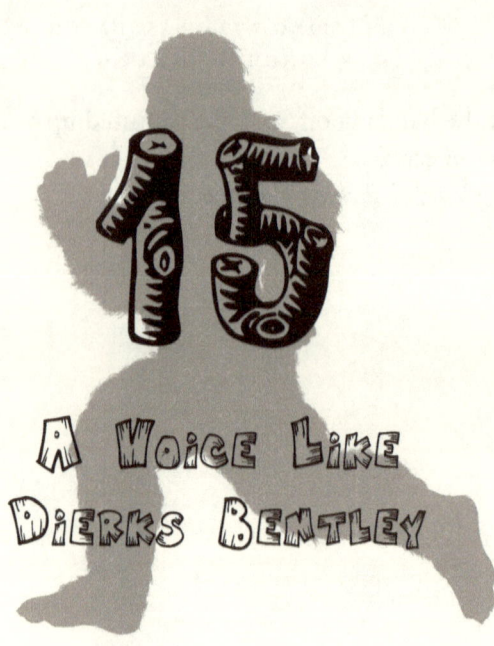

# 15

## A Voice Like Dierks Bentley

**B**if wrapped his arms around Frankie, catching his breath. He was normal again, but the elation of taking her did the trick. Pulling away, he wanted her to see him, the real him. She had played along and as he throbbed inside her warmth, unwilling to leave, he wanted to slow down. Brushing the hair from her eyes, she looked up at him in wonder.

"I don't understand," She whispered, searching his eyes for the answer.

"Understand what?" he smirked, lifting an eyebrow knowing what she meant.

"You're gorgeous."

He throbbed inside her, before leaning down to whisper, "So are you."

Bif pressed his lips hard against hers. He had been so afraid to do so in his other form, but now he could open himself up to her wandering hands and eyes. Her warm hands rippled across his ribs and glided over his collarbone. She moaned as

64

he pressed his hip against hers, grinding slowly and with skilled rhythm. Frankie's fingers tangled in his curly, blonde locks and her tongue thrust between his lips.

He let her in, both moaning as the sunlight beat down on them. Birds chirped, the fire crackled, and the bench creaked under their weight. He sucked on her tongue, and she struggled to take it back. When she broke loose, he chased it back into the warmth of her mouth. Twisting and rubbing against each other until she began sucking on his tongue.

Her knees rose higher, pressing against his ribs and opening herself further. Bif broke off the kiss to arch his back, pulling all the way out and sliding slow and steady back into place. Her breath caught in her throat; their eyes locked as he repeated the motion. Goosebumps rippled across her skin, and he could feel that low rumble of a purr escape him.

"How on earth could a man not make love to you, Frankie." It was a fact that fell from his lips.

She bit her bottom lip, and a look of uncertainty crossed her eyes.

"Don't you ever dare doubt yourself." He picked up speed, hooking a knee over her leg and shifting the angle of his cock as he stroked. "You're gorgeous, you're strong, and..." Her back started to arch as her heat tightened around him and he ground against her. "...I would love to make love to you all day and all night, Darling."

Her fingers dug into his arms, egging him on. Bif abandoned holding her leg, the pink nipples tempting his lustful appetite. He dove his arms under her and pulled her up to him, wrapping his lips around her nipple and began sucking. Frankie only clawed at his shoulders more, moaning and rocking in sync with him. Again, the growling purr rolled out of him, and he let it.

*She's as sweet as any fruit plucked in its prime. I could do this all day just to hear her moan, feel her cling to me, feel how tight she is around my cock.*

"Frankie..." He moaned her name, licking across her collarbone and up her neck. "Frankie..."

"Oh, you have a voice like Dierks Bentley," he sucked on her earlobe. "I could listen to you coo my name like that..."

Her breath caught as she lay on her back, Bif's body swallowing hers. "Bif!"

"Frankie... I've fallen for you."

She shuddered and a shriek of ecstasy erupted from her. He moaned. The pulsing heat brought him over his own edge. He pulled her close with one arm and propped himself up with the other. Her arms gripped him, and they held each other, panting.

*No man can go twice like that... that part's all thanks to being a shifter. Wait, does this count as one round or two?*

He eased her back and pulled away. Grunting, he looked for his cargo shorts. As he put them on, he reached into his tent and pulled out a blanket. Frankie was still humming and laying on the bench table and he couldn't contain his chuckle. As she sat up, he wrapped her up in the blanket.

Bif leaned down and picked up her bright pink string bikini. "You seriously didn't pack anything else?"

Frankie's eyes darted away. "I had other plans ... that were more on par with not wearing anything at all for the whole weekend."

Bif's smirk came back. "I can help you with that too."

Her eyes met his and he gave her a wink.

"Hold up, I think I can take care of the other issue too. I camp a lot, so I know the value of some extra clean clothes." Bif dug into his backpack, pulling out another pair of shorts and a long-sleeve shirt. "They might be a little big."

"It's more than what Ted packed." She wiggled off the bench, pulling the cover tighter around her. "I'm sorry…"

"Sorry?" Bif let her take the clothes from him and gauged her expression. "Girlie, there's nothing to be ashamed of."

Again, Frankie darted her eyes away. She grabbed the clothes and turned. Taking a step, she halted as if unable to make a decision on how to perform the task of getting dressed. Bif's heart swelled, aching against his chest. She jolted as his arms wrapped around her from behind. His lips tickled at her ear, and she leaned into him.

"My things are your things. You can dress and rest up in the tent and I'll make us something to eat."

A long sigh escaped her, the tension leaving her body. "I'd like that, Bif. I'd like that a lot."

He nuzzled her neck and kissed it. "Has anyone ever told you, you smell like the sweetest batch of peaches?"

She laughed, spinning around to kiss him. "No, but I'll take your word for it."

Bif let her go and she climbed into his tent. Taking in a deep breath, he turned to the cooler. There wasn't much to choose from as he shifted the items around. A slab of ham and a chunk of Cuban bread would have to do the trick. Throwing a few logs on the fire, he coaxed it back to life so it could heat the cast iron skillet.

He could hear Frankie rustling around. The smell of peaches filled the air as the blanket fell away from her bare skin. A shudder rolled through him, and he tried to focus on the task at hand but failed. As the clothes baring his scent covered her, a wave of arousal took his breath away. It was like marking what was his and it startled him.

Pulling his cell phone out of his pocket, he cursed under his breath. The battery was getting low. Despite it, he texted Satch.

[Bif: How territorial are we talking about?]

Bif tossed the ham on the skillet, the smell erupting and cutting his agony short.

*I can't believe how strong all these animal instincts are getting. Normally this sort of thing happens in shift but... I'm normal now.*

The cell phone buzzed.

[Sasshole: Very.]

[Bif: wtf does very mean?]

[Sasshole: Throw a man through a tree or tent very.]

[Bif: I need you to get me out of here. I'm gonna kill a hunter at this rate over a girl!]

As Bif hit send, the cell phone beeped and starting the shut-down process.

"Shit." His heart pounded against his chest, deafening his ears. "What the hell am I going to do?"

*Throw a man? Really, Satch? Is that the reason why the fuck you abandoned me and haven't been back? You dick. You know what's happening to me and you're just going to let me blindly fumble through it all. Fuck! I don't even know how long I have before I change back!*

"HEY!" Ted's voice echoed through the forest as he came bursting through the underbrush.

Bif tensed, the sizzling of meat on a skillet filled the space between them. His foot stepped onto the pink bikini bottoms to hide them. It was one of the few moments in his life that he was thankful for his monstrous footprint. His eyes darted about, looking for the top but spotted it tangled in Ted's shirt on the other side of the tent. At least from there, as long as Ted didn't walk any further forward, he'd never see them.

"Have... Have..." Ted panted, out of breath from the burst of energy he had exerted.

*Steroid junkie.*

Bif snorted, flipping the ham on the skillet and eyeing the tent. Frankie seemed more like a rabbit caught in the open. He couldn't let him have her. Fear came off her in waves, thick enough Bif could taste it on his tongue. He shifted, trying to swallow down the rising anger. For any man to make a woman feel that afraid...

"Have you seen a girl out here?"

Bif laughed. "Yours or mine?"

*I was never good at lying, but clever with my words.*

Ted made a face. "Mine, you Jackass!"

"In that case, nope." Bif shrugged and nodded to the tent. "Look if you don't mind, my girl's sleeping and I'm still making lunch."

"R-right." Ted backed away, throwing up his hands. "Sorry, uh, if you see a girl in a pink bikini, just let me know. I'm just on the other side of this batch of trees." He spun on his heels and jogged back from where he came.

Bif slumped forward on his knees, blowing out the breath he had held. Eyeing the tent, Frankie opened the flap, trembling.

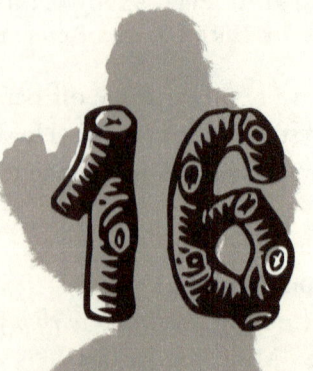

# 16
## Tent Revival

**F**rankie crawled into Bif's tent and zipped it closed. She sat there, her body still buzzing from one of the most fulfilling sex sessions she'd ever had. On the other hand, her emotions were causing chaos in her mind. She looked down at the clothes in her hand, unsure whether to be relieved or frightened.

*What the hell am I doing? Really, Frankie? Rebound sex right after a fight and with some stranger in the woods! Have I lost my mind?*

Looking over her shoulder, the silhouette of Bif made her heart ache and her body excited.

*What do I have to lose? I've only known Bif less than...* Her stomach knotted. *Twelve hours tops. Dammit, that man out there has shown me more compassion than Ted has in weeks. Made me breakfast, is making me lunch, and he even gave me clothes. I don't know why he's out here camping alone, but I take it as a sign.*

She let the blanket slide off her shoulders and started pulling on Bif's clothes. They swamped her, a little bigger than Ted's even. The shorts were sliding off her hips and being commando didn't make it feel any less awkward. Looking around she realized her bikini was outside, thrown to the wind in their moment of passion. Tugging on the pants, she reached to unzip the tent.

"HEY!" Ted's voice made her fall back on her ass.

He sounded pissed and Frankie froze.

*What am I going to say to him? He's not exactly known for being levelheaded and even-tempered. Oh no, Bif is out there. What if he tells him I'm here? Would he do that? He wouldn't, would he? What does it matter to him? He got what he wanted...*

Frankie bit her lip and started to shake. She had never been in the crossfire of two raging bulls, but at this moment, she saw horns pointed at her from both sides. Her heart pounded in her ears and fear shook her body.

*Oh my God, what have I gotten myself into?*

"Have you seen a girl out here?" She cringed at Ted's question.

*This is it. You reap what you sow, that's what Mama always said. Here it is...*

"Yours or mine?" Bif laughed and it caught her off guard.

*What kind of question is that?*

"Mine, you Jackass!" Ted sounded furious.

*Who else would he be looking for?*

Panic filled Frankie. Her situation wasn't exactly peachy, and now it just seemed to be getting worse.

"In that case, nope." Bif's words came in a wave of relief to Frankie.

*Was he testing Ted? Is Bif shielding me from him? Wait, is he implying I'm his girl now?*

Frankie looked down at the baggy shirt and shorts. They smelled like Bif, and a revelation hit her. She didn't once relish Ted's scent. Not when he tossed the shirt in her face, or any time before this awful weekend hit.

*Why am I with Ted? So what if the sex was great...* Her thoughts faltered. *Well, after Bif, it's subpar at best. Always focused on him getting off and leaving me put away wet. What kind of miserable sex life is that?*

"Look if you don't mind, my girl's sleeping and I'm still making lunch." Bif's words made her smile, and though she still shook with fear, she knew he wouldn't let Ted touch her unless she indicated otherwise.

She held her breath, waiting for Ted to stomp off. After his footsteps faded, she unzipped the tent. Swallowing, she forced herself to look up at Bif, unsure if he would be angry or frustrated with her. Her breath caught. His blue eyes bright in the sunlight and his toothy smile greeting her. And it made her heart ache.

*Ted has never looked at me like that. Not in a way that says 'he loves me' or even made me feel wanted.*

"Who are you?" The words fell from her lips as she held his pants up on her hip.

"Besides my name being Bif?" He lifted an eyebrow at her.

"Sorry, that was rude..." She searched his eyes a moment. "Thank you."

"For what?" He snorted, turning back to flip the ham once more. "It's no big deal to cook lunch for two."

"Not just that." She came closer, sitting on the bench so she could hold her arms. "What you did there, with Ted."

Bif stayed silent, eyes locked on the skillet.

"I didn't realize how scared he makes me feel until..." She gripped Bif's bicep, calling his eyes to hers. "This might be brash, but I think I'm falling for you. It's wild, and insane... But the way you make love and look—"

His lips locked with hers. She moaned, cupping the chiseled jaws and dove deeper into his mouth. Sucking on his tongue as it dared to push back into her mouth, he moaned. Frankie wanted him, wanted him inside her, wanted to go home with him, and most of all, wanted him in her life. This was a man that rarely could be found, gorgeous and passionate. She broke the kiss.

"I'll need to sneak back and get my things. I want to go home with you." If it hadn't been clear she'd cut ties with Ted, it was clear now.

"One problem." Bif sighed, tucking a strand of blonde hair behind Frankie's ear. "My phone died, and that means my ride won't be here any time soon."

Frankie collapsed on him, laughing. "Is that why you're out here? You're stranded?"

"You can say that." Bif wrapped an arm around her, chuckling. "Let's eat lunch. Satch will eventually make it out here."

"Satch?" She scooted over as he placed the ham on bread and began cutting the sandwich in half.

"A good friend of mine." He handed over her portion. "Sorry, it's just bread and meat, but it's at least filling."

"It's better than Ted's collection of Chicken Fajita MREs." Taking a bite, she relished in the fact she had been given real food twice now by this amazing man before her.

"Wait, isn't that in the top ten worst flavors?" Bif paused before taking a bite. "You don't think he bought them up because they were on sale at the army surplus store, do you?"

She swallowed her food. "They probably offered them to him for free. It was horrible, I gagged on it, but he eats them up. I swear the man has no taste buds."

Bif started laughing, trying not to choke on his food. "You might be onto something."

They ate in silence for a while. Bif finished first and began cleaning out the skillet and she had taken her last bite, unable to finish. She stared at the sandwich for a while before turning to watch Bif for a moment. Her self-esteem wavered once more and as if he could sense it, he turned to her with a confused look on his face.

"You ok, Frankie?" Bif sat up, giving her his full attention.

"You must think horribly of me," she muttered, her chest stinging.

"Why would I?" His distraught expression went through her, but before she could continue, he scooped her into his arms. "If anyone should be horrible, it's me. I mean, trying to sneak in on another man's girl like I did but... but..."

"I was the one who came marching into your camp, eating your food, offering myself up like some prost—" He squeezed her tighter, cutting her words off.

His voice was low, rumbling in her ear. "Did you mean it when you said you wanted to go home with me?"

She clung onto his bareback, never wanting to let go. "Yeah, I did."

"Let's get your shit from Ted's camp then." He kissed the top of her head and her heart leapt to her throat. "You're my girl. Let me show you how a man should treat his girl. Let me take care of you, Frankie."

Tears welled up in Frankie's eyes.

"Uh, but we still have the issue of being out here until my friend arrives. Hope you like camping." She started laughing, sniffling. "Unless you have some way to charge a phone."

"I do!" She pulled away, wiping the tears from her cheeks. "But we'll need to wait for Ted to leave camp."

"Well, he's now out hunting Big Foot and you, so I don't think he's gonna be staying in camp much." Bif wiped a remaining tear off her face with his thumb.

"Is it a micro-USB?" She stood up, tugging his pants up. "The Bronco is unlocked, and my charger is in there."

"Perfect." He stood and began heading toward camp.

She paled, "Wait, he just left here."

"Oh, he's back fix... um, checking his trail cams," Bif corrected himself and Frankie furrowed her brow at him. "It's now or never, Girlie."

"R-right." She caught up to him, curious now. "But how do you know?"

He gave her a nervous side glance. "I've been camping for a long time; you catch onto these sorts of things."

Frankie wasn't buying it. "Hold up." She managed to run ahead and stand in his way, palms flat on his bare chest. "I can't help but think you're hiding something."

Bif's eyes widened. "Like what?"

"Why you're really out here." Frankie gave him a serious glare.

"Look, I got shitfaced during our campout, and they thought it funny to leave me behind," Bif confessed.

"Oh." Frankie lifted her hands and let him pass her. "But who doesn't get shitfaced at a party?"

"It's not the normal routine for me." They came to the clearing and as he had predicted, no signs of Ted.

"Oh?" Making it to the Bronco, he slid into the driver's side and she the passenger seat. "Why is that?"

Bif flinched, pausing a minute before pulling his phone and plugging it in. "I recently broke up with someone."

Frankie's mind spun. *What were the chances of two heartbroken people meeting in the woods and hooking up?*

"Look, I'm not hooking up with you for a rebound." His tone and expression were serious. "She was bad news, and the sort my friends warned me about. I should have listened. To her, I was a free ride until she found what she really wanted, and that happened a few days ago."

*This must be fate...* Frankie sighed, the last of her tension and doubts melting away.

# 17

## Bronco Fun

**B**if waited for her response, but Frankie gave him a tender smile. Her eyes said it all. She felt bad for him and could relate. She had just broken it off with Ted after all, but to know he was in the same situation made them closer somehow. The muscles in her body lost their tension, and in turn, he could let his own fall from his shoulders. Looking back to his phone, it was charging at last, with fast charging initiated.

"How long will it take?" Frankie had changed topics.

"Says an hour and seventeen minutes if I keep it turned off," Bif announced.

"Okay." Frankie bent down to gather the things on the floor. "Dammit, Ted."

"What's wrong?" Bif furrowed his brow.

"Asshole dumped my purse out." She shifted her position to better reach the floorboard.

Watching her, she was on all fours on top of the bench seat. Ass staring at him, her head and hands scrambled to gather her things and place them back into the large satchel purse. Bif licked his lips, his pants tight as his cock grew hard. He panted, hot with arousal, shifting himself in anticipation of what he wanted to do with her. Reaching out to grab his pants off her hip, he watched his hand shift from normal to hairy.

*FUCK! NOT NOW! I'm in the fucking Bronco with her and if she turns around, I'm so fucked!!!*

The smell of peaches brought his attention back to Frankie's ass. "Don't move. Stay there and don't look."

"Wait, what?" Frankie banged her head on the dashboard, her eyes squeezing shut.

"I can't stand watching you wiggle your ass in my face like this," he breathed, tugging his shorts off her ass and to her knees. "Just a taste..."

"Bif!" She braced herself on the floor. "What about Ted?"

"Better keep your head and voice down." He relished in the heat of her skin under his hands. "You think you can keep the screams in?"

"Oh god..." Frankie's arousal rattled through her, and Bif could sense the heat in her body rising. "You're seriously going to fuck me in Ted's Bronco?"

His fingers slid over her fold, already wet and hot. "Yeah, because I doubt he's ever finished the job."

Frankie's heart sped up, her anger rising. "How would you know?"

Bif purred, "Because Ted's that kind of douchebag to finger a girl just long enough to get head."

*That one hit a nerve. She tensed up, even white knuckled. I called it.*

Frankie shifted, straddling her legs to give him better access. "You're assuming you can make me scream."

Bif laughed, unzipping his pants to relieve his hard, throbbing cock. He could see the shudder roll through her, the excitement growing between them. A smile filled Bif's face, and he wondered what he wanted to do first. Even knowing the quicker he came the faster he changed back; he didn't want to short-change her in pleasure. His fingers slid from her knee and up her inner thigh. The prickling of her skin and the growing smell of peaches let him know she was growing ripe with want. Gripping her hips, he slid her across the bench seat quickly, making her yelp.

"You've lost." His hot cock rubbed against the opening of her pussy. "I think that's a record for me."

"That's not fair." She squirmed and his cock throbbed against her. "Dammit you're so hard and big."

Bif leaned over her, his hands sliding from her hips and finding her breasts. He enjoyed how her curvy body fit into his own like a lost piece of himself. Her breasts soft, nipples hard, and the dripping of her onto his dick were intoxicating. Frankie's head started to turn to look back and Bif panicked. He slammed his cock inside her, forcing her to focus on keeping herself from faceplanting on the floor. She whimpered but bit her lip.

*Oh, she's so tight and hot right now! Smells like a peach cobbler on a summer day, and I want it all to myself!*

He squeezed her breasts harder, twisting her nipples. Again, a muffled whimper. Rocking his hips, long hard strokes earned shaking of legs and muffled screeches. Bif wanted to make her scream. One hand abandoned its breast, snaking down the middle of her torso and diving between her thighs. She squirmed and he could smell the mixture of panic and excitement. This would be hard for her to keep quiet.

Pulling out, he plunged a finger inside her, coming back to circle her clit with ease. She let out a gasp, as if coming up for air before diving back to silence herself. Her legs started to close, and he threw his knee between them, nudging them back open. The shudder that rocked her body egged him on. Teasing, he rubbed the tip of his dick on the opening. Again, she tried to close her legs, moaning in a wave of agony and pleasure. He rushed forward, thrusting his length into her.

Frankie arched her back, but his reflexes had been quick. Abandoning the breast, he gripped her shoulder to keep her from banging her head on the dash. Bif cursed under his breath, shifting back to normal as his peak slammed into him. The break in focus made him moan, his other hand abandoning her thighs to grip the seat. He started to come. His cock was hard as she tightened more around him. Frozen from the hard hit of his orgasm, she began grinding against him and he moaned. His hands came back to her hips, wanting to rock in tandem with her.

"What if I make you scream?" Bif realized she had been watching him, though unaware if she had seen the shift. "You seem to be the noisy one."

"Ha, I didn't almost bang my head on the dashboard twice." He swallowed the uncertainty down.

She managed to pull her top half back out of the floorboard. She rolled back on her heels, and he relished that she sat on his lap, never letting him slide out of her. She began rocking, playing with herself as she ground in his lap. Again, a moan and purr rolled out of him.

"I love it when you make that sound," Bif's face flashed red. *If only she knew I wasn't doing that until I met her...*

He slid his hands across her body, wanting to feel every muscle at work. The way she rocked, the shaking in her legs, and the firmness of her breasts. She hadn't come yet. He hadn't won the contest though the Bronco's rusted suspension had started creaking from all their fun. She moaned, and he could feel her tighten on his dick and a shudder rolled through her. He hated seeing her agonize on the edge of orgasm.

"Turn around," he muttered.

"I thought you didn't want me looking at you?" She pulled away; the cold air unbearable compared to her heat. "You're such a strange one, Bif."

"I could say the same about you, Frankie." She smirked, spinning around to mount him, his cock sliding deep inside her.

"Is this what you wanted?" Their eyes locked and he started to grow hard again. "I take that as a yes."

Bif wanted more. His hands slid his shorts off her body so he could see all of her. Again, his cock throbbed, and she tightened in response. She leaned down and kissed him deeply. His arms wrapped around her, fingers riding in the divot of her spine. Tongues lashed at one another, taking turns chasing. Frankie began rocking once more, moaning into his mouth. He broke the kiss, wanted to watch her work, shifting them both so he could slide deeper inside her.

"I can't play with myself like this." Her cheeks flushed; her orgasm so close yet too far to reach. "I want to come so bad..."

"Why would you need to play with yourself when you have me?"

Pulling her into him, his lips wrapped around a nipple. Hard short sucks sent her body into a shiver. His other hand rode her spine down, gripping her ass hard. She tightened. He began thrusting in and out of her fast and hard. She whimpered. A yelp started to form. Swallowing only made her whimper. An orgasm like no other peaked. Desperation took hold. Frankie lunged forward, her teeth biting into his shoulder. It muffled a scream and he moaned.

*My god she's like an animal and I want to drink from it all day!*

She came, a gush of fluid escaping her as nails and teeth dug into him. It did nothing to slow him. He wanted her to come hard, he wanted her to scream his name. He pulled her off, and before Frankie knew why, she found herself on all fours on the bench seat. Without wasting time, Bif was inside her, fucking her doggie style. The deep hard strokes made her breath catch as she gripped the door's arm rest. His hand rolled over her hip, playing with her clit and she yelped.

*Close, but I want to hear that scream!*

# 18

## Left Hanging

**F**rankie's eyes were wide. She had wanted to be fucked in this Bronco for so long and at last it had happened. The only odd thing, it wasn't Ted grinding away at her backside or playing with her clit. Nor would she change a single thing of what had unfolded. Her breasts swayed with each powerful thrust from Bif, and she would start losing the game of keeping quiet. Granted, she had noticed how he moaned when she tightened.

*He feels so fucking amazing!*

Moaning seemed to be neutral ground, but the man had moves and a cock to back it. Her thighs were wet, her body wanting him more. A shiver shook her, the arousal still climbing under the heat of his body. Her eyes fell to her purse and there she saw her secret weapon: high dollar lubricant. She reached down, moaning as his dick rubbed inside her in a way that made her legs numb. She gave herself away, and he made his thrusting slow and strong. It was enough to almost make her forget why'd she'd shifted her body. He picked up speed and she held her breath.

*I can't lose! I want to hear him scream my name this time!*

Desperate, she tossed it behind her. Bif halted his barrage when it hit him in the chest. The cold bottle fell, resting on her ass cradled where they joined. He picked it up to read the label. Confusion struck his face and she smirked. Frankie saw how he flushed; he was starting to lose ground already with that face.

"You ain't dry, so are you proposing what I think you are?" One eyebrow arched high as he wiggled the bottle in his hand. "Didn't think you were that kind of gal, Frankie."

"One of us will be screaming the other's name before we leave this Bronco." She wiggled, tightening to make him moan. "And it's not going to be me, Bif. I already lost once."

He narrowed his eyes at her, reflecting the playful smile she gave him. "Are you sure about that?"

Frankie went to wiggle again, but he pulled out. He had evaded her next attack. A yelp escaped her as Bif flipped her over on her back. The bulk of his body weighed down on her and she found herself nose to nose with him. She searched his eyes and he seemed to be doing the same. She moved to kiss him and lifted his face away, denying her.

*What was that? Lure me in with those baby blues and denied.*

"What's wrong?" she whispered, her voice barely audible over her own heartbeat.

*Is he against it? Was I too bold? I didn't think... I mean, I barely know the man and I'm assuming...*

"You don't have to go so far to please me." His voice rolled into her ear in a deep, low grumble. "I'm not him, I..."

*He thinks I'm trying to please him! Normally, it would be a yes but this time... this time...*

"It was in my purse for me. I want ... it," she confessed then bit her lip.

*Am I out of my mind? Why'd I let the cat out of the bag so bluntly?*

He closed his eyes. "You really were looking for a weekend fuckfest with your man. How'd he not know?"

*EXACTLY!*

"It was his idea originally." Frankie couldn't stop her face from turning red with embarrassment and frustration.

"Oh. I guess he forgot but…" He leaned in, the heat of his breath on her ear. "Good thing I'm here. I'm more than happy to take care of you."

*I would die happy to hear his voice whisper in my ear like this every night.*

He began kissing her neck and working his way down. Pausing at her collarbone, he sucked on it until he left a hickey before trailing down to her nipple. There he sucked long and hard, teeth teasing her before he let go with a pop. Frankie watched him as his lips travelled across the hills and valleys of her body. Those piercing blue eyes magical as they stole glances, meeting her eyes at key moments. Her skin pimpled as he pecked across her abdomen, a barren land often left out in intimate times.

Frankie's breath caught. His head dove between her thighs.

*Oh no! Not after…*

Lips and tongue hot around her swollen clit. She arched, whimpering to keep in the scream that pained to be released. The purr and moan from him made her knees jerk high, his shoulders keeping her legs from closing around him. She couldn't recall ever getting oral so far into a fuck session, but oh how sensitive it had become. Her fingers gripped his hair, trying to pull him from her. At this rate she would lose their contest of endurance. Her teeth dug into her tongue, denying the need to scream, to beg Bif to stop, beg him to do more, beg him to… It only coaxed Bif to take a long lick across her throbbing pussy before suckling on her again. The shaking in her legs made it impossible to hide how amazing he felt. She panted, trying to catch her breath from the waves of exhilaration filling her.

*I'm drowning in pleasure!*

"It's no fair..." She pleaded, hiding her face under her forearm. "You've broken that part."

The suction broke, making her jolt. "And you think what you offered was fair, Darling?"

"It was even ground."

"Is that so?" A finger dove inside her pussy, stroking in just the right angle. "You're telling me you like this as much as..." It slid out and into her ass and she gasped. Her back arched and she moaned. "Oh, I guess I'll take that as a yes."

"Please..." She peered down at him, and he narrowed his eyes once more. "Please give it to me."

"Oh, that's just playing dirty, begging me like that while wearing a face I can't say no to."

Bif grabbed the bottle and began rubbing down his long, hard cock. Frankie's heart raced, her breath quickening. Another squirt of the bottle and he pushed two fingers inside her ass. She wanted anal; her last boyfriend failing, and the one before that ruining it for her. It excited her to orgasm to have a man not take her once, but twice. Normally she offered it to the men in her life she hoped would be around for something longer than a one-night stand, but with Bif...

*I can't leave here without knowing what it would be like to be fucked by this man in every way possible. Is it wrong I want to go home with him and not Ted? A fucking stranger I met in the forest has been...*

He leaned forward, the tip of his dick pressing against the slick opening of her ass. "Are you sure? I ain't small, lady."

Frankie wrapped her arms around him, pulling him forward. It was enough to make him enter her. They moaned as he slid slowly, deeper into her until he was all the way inside.

Frankie lifted her knees, giving him better access. He leaned down, kissing her deep and hard. Again, their tongues chased one another. Frankie would suck on his, holding him captive. Both moaned into one another's mouths as he began to rock his hips. They were holding back their screams of pleasure as they refused to break the kiss.

The glass hatch of the Bronco creaked open. Bif let most of his weight fall onto Frankie, and he signaled for her to be quiet.

"Fucking Frankie. I bet she trashed these cameras. Dammit, when I get my hands on her…"

They were far enough down to be covered by the bench seat.

The sound of equipment being thrown into the bed of the truck. "And just when I was seeing signs of a Sasquatch in the area. I need to get that asshole and his girlfriend next door out of here."

Frankie lipped, "I'm your girlfriend?"

Bif made a goofy face, "Why not?"

"Maybe I should throw their tent on their fire." Ted threw more cameras in the back. "I could hear them fucking this morning … and I'm sure they spooked Sasquatch with the way his girl was screeching."

Frankie's brow furrowed; anger written across her face. "Asshole."

Bif lifted his eyebrows high, "Don't look at me so angry."

As the blood rushed to her face, she lipped, "Fuck Ted.'"

A hand slid across her hip and gripped her ass cheek. Bif had a sparkle in his eyes. He leaned on her, starting to rock his hips once more. Her fingers dug into his shoulders. The speed of it increasing just enough to keep her in a never-ending arch without making the Bronco rock. She heard more equipment slam into the back of the truck, and she tightened on Bif's cock. He grunted. She opened her mouth to tell him to stop, but he tucked his face into her shoulder. Shivers shook her as his breath hit her neck like hot wax.

Bif whispered, smooth and sultry in tone, "Fuck me."

The glass hatch slammed close. "Frankie! Where the fuck are you!"

"Harder," she breathed.

"As you wish."

The Bronco started to rock, though slightly. Bif pulled up, looking out the windows. A big smile stretched across his face. Sitting up, she loved how he looked down at her naked body like a hungry beast. Her body shuddered, cold without him on top of her, without her breasts against the wall of muscle. His fingers dug into her hips, and he banged her with renewed vigor, the Bronco threatening to squeak as it had done at the start of this game of theirs. She arched, her hands only able to clutch his arms, nails clawing. He began moaning, his cock hardening inside her. An eruption of heat filled her as he came inside.

She lost her composure, "FUCK ME BIF!"

His fingers let go, trailing between her thighs. Fingers dove inside her wet, swollen pussy as he still throbbed inside her ass. She squealed, wiggling as a thumb circled her clit and fingers thrust in and out.

"BIF!" At last, she lost.

Her warmth tightened on his finger, on his cock, and the gush of her orgasm sent her heart aching against her chest.

*My god, I've never come so hard in all my life.*

Her breasts heaved as she fought to catch her breath. A tune caught their attention. Bif's phone booted on as it hit full battery. Pulling away from each other, Frankie gave him Ted's shirt to clean up with, and they laughed.

# 19

## Camp Disaster

**B**if zipped up his pants and grinned at Frankie. His secret nearly blown, yet neither of them realized how far they would go even when Ted came back. Wiping sweat from his brow, he looked around. There had been no sign or scent of Ted. Unplugging his cell phone, Bif started his text to Satch. He hit send and watched as Frankie tried to wiggle back into his shorts.

[Bif: Come get me.]

He yanked the backside up and she laughed as they slid on at last. Her face flushed and she hid away, putting on his shirt. Bif shifted and pulled the bottle of lube out from behind him. He nudged Frankie's arm with it. Puffing out her cheeks, she grabbed it and shoved it into her purse. Bif's phone vibrated in his hands, and he turned his attention to the screen.

[Sasshole: Why?]

[Bif: Look, the hunter guy is hot on my tail, and we're stranded out here. COME GET US!]

[Sasshole: Us?]

[Bif: Me and my]

He paused and looked at Frankie as she took inventory of her things. She blinked and looked over at him, confused.

"Is there something on my face?" She dug through her items. "Where's that compact mirror?"

"No, you're fine." Bif rubbed the back of his neck, looking at the unfinished text. "Did you mean it when you said you wanted to come home with me?"

Frankie froze and inhaled deeply. She held it there for some time before meeting his eyes. Bif swallowed. Her face so stern, eyes bright, and she gripped her purse tight. He raised his eyebrows as the anxiety built between them, both wearing a face asking themselves an array of questions. Doubts building, Bif opened his mouth, but she slid across the bench seat, the heat of her body and smell of peaches pulling at the Big Foot inside him.

She whispered, "Did you mean it when you told Ted I was your girl?"

He smirked, "You heard that?"

She nodded.

"I meant it as long as you want the title." He brushed a lock of hair off her forehead, clearing his view of her face.

"I want it. I want to be your girlfriend." Her cheeks blossomed red. "It sounds so stupid... we've barely met and... and..." Tears were building in her eyes.

"Stop that." His voice, low and soft. "I came on to you. Even though you were clearly with someone. You don't have to come home with me. I can give you a ride home, so you don't have to deal with that douchebag Ted."

"No," she looked pained. "I think I really do want to go home with you."

"Okay." He kissed her forehead.

Turning back to his phone, he finished the message he had started.

[Bif: Me and my girlfriend.]

Hitting send, he opened the Bronco and helped her out. They started working their way back to their camp when they heard a commotion. The sound of grunting and huffing, like a wild animal, startled them. Bif and Frankie squatted in the underbrush. There in Bif's camp, Ted was running a hunting knife through the tent. He turned and kicked over the cooler. Reaching into the torn apart tent, he gripped a bright pink bikini top. His face turned purple with rage.

"Oh no." Frankie started to shake. "He knows! I'm so sorry Bif... I..."

Growling came out of Bif, angry like a rabid dog.

"Are you okay?" Frankie's hands wrapped around his arm, and he regained his focus.

"Fuck." The territorial rage had blinded all rational thought.

Bif lifted his cell phone and snapped a photo as Ted threw Frankie's bikini on the fire. As he texted Satch, he pulled Frankie along behind him. Ted would be shredding his camp for a while. The only relief is the ground rules all shifters had on the night of a shift; don't bring any forms of identification. Ted could look all he wanted, but there wouldn't be a single clue as to who he was or anyone who had camped there a few night before.

[Satch: Is that dude throwing a pink bikini in the fire?]

[Bif: WE NEED A RIDE NOW!]

[Satch: FUCK! On my way... what the hell did you do?]

[Bif: I fucked the Sasquatch Hunter's girlfriend and she's coming home with me!!!!]

[Satch: Dude, I've told you before, fucking a girl doesn't make them your girlfriend.]

[Bif: COME FUCKING GET ME! I'M GETTING TERRITORIAL!]

[Satch: ... eta a few hours.]

They came out into the opening where the Bronco sat. Frankie started pacing, holding her head. Bif mind spun circles.

Normally dealing with something like this wasn't no problem, but with newfound animal instincts overriding logic, he'd have to keep his distance.

"Shit, shit, shit!" Frankie had tears running down her cheeks. "I'm so sorry, Bif."

"Calm down." He wasn't sure if it was meant for her or himself. "We have a few hours before my ride will be here."

Frankie looked at him with dread. "Hours? It'll be dark."

"Yeah, I know."

"FRANKIE!" Ted's voice made them both flinch.

Bif grabbed her hand, pulling her into the woods opposite the direction of his camp. They turned and twisted until he found a small clearing with a downed pine tree. He eyed the area, seeing no signs that Ted had ventured back there as of late. Frankie squeezed his hand hard as a shudder rattled through her. He turned to her and hugged her tightly against him. Hot tears hit the bare skin of his chest and anger rose up inside him.

*Ted will pay for this ... somehow, some way.*

"I'm sorry I dragged you into this," she sobbed, pressing into him more as if hungry to take in all the protection and security he had to offer. "He's always been an asshole but to see him coming unglued..."

Bif shushed her, rubbing her shoulder as he kissed the top of her head. "It's okay! You did nothing wrong. You came out here to spend time with someone you love..."

Bif choked on his words, flashes of Bethany from last month sneaking into his mind.

*Wasn't this me just last month? Wanting to just have a good time and be intimate and she blew me off even at camp? Am I any different than Frankie?*

"I thought I loved Ted." Frankie's words made his heart flutter. "But then I discovered someone I wanted more, that I didn't think existed at all. I know I've been a complete whore and brash but, but..."

He chuckled, rocking her to calm her down. "To be fair, Frankie. Just last month I was in your boat... out here in fact. Thought she was the one or at least someone I'd be with for a while. In the end, I felt used, hurt, and broken even just a few nights ago. I sat there at camp feeling sorry for myself. Good thing my friends left me out her, or we'd never have crossed paths."

She laughed, pulling away to look him in the eyes. "Maybe life just brought us together when we needed each other the most."

He smiled. "I like that idea."

In the distance, they could hear Ted calling her name. She rushed forward, hugging him, and he held her a moment. Heaving a sigh, Bif had to do something. The evening sunset sky overhead began shifting into purple and orange hues. If he could just mislead Ted and get him spun around in the woods, it would buy them time to grab some things from his camp and make their way to one of the side roads.

"Look Frankie. I'm going to mislead Ted. You stay here. I'll see if my bag is still in camp; since I don't keep it right in the camp area, I might have it intact."

"What if you get lost?" She broke away, pacing and tugging on the hem of her shirt. "How are you going to find me out here? In the dark?"

A toothy grin crested between his lips. "I grew up in these woods. Trust me when I say I've had to walk out of here by myself with no ride a few times."

She searched his face for a moment and relented. "Okay, Bif. I'll trust you." She reached into his pocket and grabbed his cell phone. "But let me give you my number just in case."

The arousal waving through him at the sensation of her fingers in his front pocket made him hard again. He cursed under his breath as he struggled to unlock the phone so she could put her number into the contact list. In all the years he had been shifting, this would be unforgettable as to how much he struggled with the inner animal side. There had been stories, plenty of bullshits called, but now he had one to add to the pile.

"There." She handed it back with a half-hearted smile. "My phone doesn't work out here, but…"

"Most don't," he muttered, shaking the thoughts from his head. "Sit and wait for me. When I get back, we'll have one last romp in the woods while we wait for our ride."

He leaned down and kissed her deeply. She moaned against his lips, and he purred. Pulling away, denying the animalistic urge and the want to bend her over and have his way with her, he set his aim for Ted. The Sasquatch Hunter had proven on more than one occasion how terrible he was at navigating the woods during the day, let alone at night. He would send him in a direction he hadn't been and abandon him just far enough for him to spin in circles for a while.

Looking over his shoulder, he watched Frankie sit on the fallen tree, hugging her arms.

*She's mine and I get to take her home. I promise you'll look back at this night and only remember the good, Frankie.*

# 20

## Caught on Camera

Frankie watched Bif disappear into the trees. It startled her how fast night had fallen on them, and now she felt crazy. Here she was, waiting on a strange man with the biggest dick she'd ever had while her now ex-boyfriend, the Sasquatch Hunter, started to lose his shit like a mad man. She laughed. It all seemed like a bad B-rated porno movie at this rate. She looked down at her phone and cursed under her breath.

"I didn't get his number. Fuck."

She turned on the flashlight feature and took a look around. The small opening had very little to offer besides the downed pine she sat on. Her light reflected something at the base of a nearby tree. Curious, she wandered over to it and knelt down. Her eyes widened. It was a trail cam with "TED" etched into the side. She puffed out her cheeks, seeing red. Opening the device she found no SD card remained. Looking around she found it a good distance away.

"Thankfully they're red."

94

She looked at the items in her hand: a trail cam belonging to her ex and the SD card. A grin spread across her face as a vengeful thought came across her mind.

*If I set this up to run again, then when Bif comes back...*

Looking at the downed tree, she began looking for a good angle. She would want to keep it low to the ground in hopes of keeping Bif's face out of the shot. Her imagination pondered on what they would do, where Bif would bend her over and if she could glare into the camera and make sure when Ted reviewed the footage, he saw what he could have had.

*Here should work. At this angle, I don't think Bif will notice, but if I make him stand over there to... yeah. Yeah, Ted will have a front row ticket to the show.*

Snapping the SD card in, she flipped the switch and rushed back to the fallen pine. She checked her phone, but it beeped at her: *battery low 10%.* Soon she wouldn't even have a flashlight. All around she could hear the crickets and a whip-poor-will in the distance. The night air had cooled, moisture rising and making her skin pimple.

Her phone died at last, and she lost track of time. Part of her was drowsy, exhausted from the day's events, but the other part of her waited with wanton want. The idea of having his hands, his lips, and his tongue exploring her body again, just thinking of his hard cock inside her again, made her wet and her loins throbbed with anticipation. Her body heated at the idea, growing wet recalling the last few times and the sensations he had wracked her body with. Her hand slid under the waist of the shorts.

*These clothes are his. Even the shirt has his scent still.*

Her fingers dove between her thighs. She gasped.

*Just thinking about him makes me so damn wet!*

She began to play, her finger circling her clit. A moan escaped her, her nipples growing hard. They brushed against the fabric of the shirt, adding to her excitement. Her breath quickened. In her mind, she pulled those peaking moments forward. She peaked. Breath catching, she leaned forward moaning. Her eyes shot up to the trail cam, and she laughed. In the moment of thinking of Bif, she forgot about the idea Ted would be seeing everything that unfolded tonight.

In the distance, she heard some footsteps. She paled. Biting her lips, she waited to see who would break through the trees. After several minutes, nothing happened. She looked to her phone and cursed. A growling sound came from the underbrush and her heart skipped a beat.

*Bif's going to come back to find me mangled by a wolf or bear. Shit!*

She stood in alarm. Her eyes wide and searching.

"It's me."

Instant relief washed over her to hear Bif's voice. "Oh, thank goodness. Did you lose Ted?"

"Yeah." He sounded nervous again. "And I did find my bag in one piece."

She stood again. "Then let's go. Let's get out of here."

"First, I have a promise to fulfill." He paused. "But I need you to close your eyes."

"This again?"

Frankie snorted, bewildered by the request once more.

*Good Lord, we've fucked every way to Sunday, and he still needs me to close my eyes on the start?*

"I'm sorry. I'll explain later, but this should be the last time."

"Fine." She closed her eyes and crossed her arms.

His footsteps left the hidden spot in the trees. The heat of his body close and the amazing scent of his musky cologne filled her nose. Bif's finger brushed a strand of hair behind her ear before trailing down her neck, across her breast and torso, and stopping at the button on the shorts, unsnapping them. She gripped his hand, and he froze.

"Not yet." She whispered. "It's my turn to treat you."

"But…"

Frankie licked her lips, "I want you… I want to play with your cock like you played with my pussy, Bif. I promise, no hands."

She opened her mouth, her tongue like a red carpet inviting him to come inside. The pause lasted longer than expected, but before she could close her mouth to say anything else, the tip of his cock tapped her tongue. She fought the urge to reach up and grip his throbbing erection. Her tongue circled the cap and he moaned. He was hard and it throbbed every time the heat of her tongue slid across the bottom side.

Pausing, she suckled at the tip and another moan escaped him. He leaned forward ever slightly, and she knew she had made him weak in the knees for a moment. As he straightened his stance, she leaned forward. Slow and tongue wiggling, she took him in. The tip of his throbbing cock pressed against the back of her throat. Bif grunted, the lean in his posture letting her know what he wanted. She swallowed, deep throating him a little farther and again, he moaned.

Calculated, the tip of her tongue pressing hard against the base of his dick, she pulled herself off. When her lips left the tip, they came off with a loud pop. She began kissing the tip and suckling her way down his shaft and back up again. Each one earned her more vocal purrs and elated moans.

*Ted was never this vocal and it's making me so wet hearing Bif.*

She began sucking him in and out, taking him all the way in to the back of her throat and back to almost leaving him. His fingers tangled in her hair, thrusting along with her. Her tongue wiggled, enjoying how hard he grew, how often she could make his erection throb. She began sucking harder and holding it longer. At last, the sensation she had been waiting for, when a cock became rock hard, the ridge of the cap firm, and the tip riding the roof of her mouth.

She broke her promise, grabbing the back of his shorts to pull him all the way into her mouth. The moan as she deep throated and swallowed was enough to break the peak. A rush of heat slid down the back of her throat and she heard Bif gasp.

"Frankie!"

Inside, she smiled.

*Finally, got him to scream my name!*

Another gush and she swallowed all that he offered her before pulling away and off. She looked up at him and he panted, leaning forward and catching himself on the pine. For a moment, looking like a giant monster, but in a blink of an eye all seemed normal. Wiping her mouth, she had made him weak in the legs and he looked at her baffled.

"First time with baby deer legs?" she teased.

"I've given my fair share, but never received them."

A sparkle flashed in his eyes, and he rushed her. Arms strong and thick invaded her clothes, conquering her body. He spun her around, jerking the shorts off her ass. Gasping, he thrust inside her hard and fast. He hadn't even checked to see if she had been wet enough, but she had been drenching her own thighs as she sucked him off.

*How could he still be this hard after coming!*

She began shrieking, hoping somewhere out there, Ted could hear her pleasure. Her back arched. Bif's hands slid across her torso, each hand squeezing her breasts. Fingers pinched her nipples, and she tightened around his hard erection as it thrust in and out of her. She came, hard and wild. Her scream was visceral as it echoed through the forest. A rush of heat filled her. Bif had come again, purring and moaning into her ear. She rocked her hips against him, riding the orgasm out as long as she could.

*The camera!*

Bif pulled off her, but she grabbed his arm. With renewed vigor, she pulled him to sit on the log and she straddled him. Staring at the camera over his shoulder, she gave a toothy grin. Pulling the shirt off, she threw it off to the side. As if reading her mind, Bif took a nipple into his mouth, sucking long and hard. She pulsed her hips, marveling over how long the man could stay hard with no down time. A girl could break herself with a man like this, and she would gladly be first in line.

He moaned into her breasts, his arms wrapping around her as he thrust in rhythm with her own rocking. Gripping a fistful of his hair, she could feel another orgasm rising. She held him against her tightly, his teeth teasing her nipple making her shriek. It was enough to make her tighten on his cock, and he picked up his speed. Another squeal of delight escaped her. What he didn't see was that she never broke eye contact with the trail cam as she came once more. Another wail of passion echoed in the woods as she peaked. He leaned back, coming with her, arms tight around her to dive as deep as he could.

Panting, she collapsed forward on his shoulder. He started to laugh, kissing her neck.

"You were hungry to fuck me again, huh?"

She started to laugh. "You could say that."

"I'm not used to a girl who can keep up with me." She realized he struggled to catch his breath.

"How can you keep going after coming so hard?"

Another chuckle rolled from his chest, "It's a family secret."

"Holy shit, I could hear you two a few miles back." Satch strutted into the open.

Frankie folded into Bif who shielded her from his friend. "Dammit Satch! Don't fucking scare me like that!"

"Sorry, sorry!" He spun on his heel; hands high in the air. "Find your clothes. I won't peek."

Bif grabbed the shirt and handed it to her and gave her a moment to find the shorts she had abandoned. She reached over and grabbed her purse and nodded.

"I'm ready to go."

"Let's get the hell out of here." He grabbed her hand, fingers entwining. "Satch, let's go."

Satch shifted, eyeing Frankie from head to toe before offering a hand. "I'm Satch, Bif's best bud."

"Frankie." She shook his hand, taking note of the formal attire and loosened tie still around his neck. "Bif's girlfriend. Thanks for leaving your event to come get us."

"Event?" He looked down and covered his face. "More like escaping the Spaghetti Monster."

"Oh?" Bif lifted an eyebrow as they started to follow Satch through the woods. "Did Yeti Spaghetti find out you were dating Yvonne?"

"Oh yeah. At the family gala and let's just say it was cancelled a tad early when he shoved over an ice sculpture and flipped the buffet table."

"No joke?" Bif marveled, pulling Frankie closer as she soaked in the insane story. "Half pint has some hidden strength in those tiny limbs after all."

"Yea, Yvonne broke up with me because I wouldn't fight him for her." Satch shrugged. "What can I say? I'm a lover, not a fighter."

*What kind of people have I gotten myself involved with?*

# 21

## EPILOGUE

I t took Ted all night and half the next day to find his camp and Bronco. When he did, the tires had been slashed, his equipment destroyed, and his tent shredded. A Sasquatch had been there. The prints everywhere. Luckily his phone and laptop had come with him, and he reviewed the footage of the trail cams that hadn't been torn apart or sabotaged. Another truck pulled up and he climbed in. As they abandoned his Bronco for the time being, he flipped open his laptop to review the footage.

"What the hell happened to you, Ted?" Jay furrowed his brow.

"Sasquatch attacked the camp. Spent two days chasing the son of a bitch."

"No way." The truck turned down the dirt road leading out of the forest. "Never seen one that active. Wait, where's your girl? Thought you took her with you this time?"

"She fucking left with some guy camping next to us."

"Holy fuck." Jay scratched his beard. "You've had one fucked up camping trip."

"Tell me about it. I just hope I caught something on camera."

As he flicked through footage of insects triggering the motion sensor, he suddenly came across a shot of Frankie's face. He swallowed. As he reviewed the footage, wishing he had bought the trail cams with audio recording, he endured. The next video he watched as she masturbated in clear view of the camera. How he hated seeing the rebellious glare on her face. She was pissed.

Clicking on the next video, he paled. There he saw what he had been searching for but also... He covered his mouth watching Frankie suck the dick on Big Foot and as he came, he shifted into a man. From there he grew ill. The way he made love to her made him jealous and they changed positions. From there, it was as if he locked eyes with Frankie as another man, no BIG FOOT with the BIG COCK, fucked his girl the way she had wanted him to fuck her. She flicked a bird, grinning wildly before she arched and came. He recognized her body language.

"Ted, I said did you get anything good?" Jay's voice cut through at last.

"No." Bile rolled into Ted's throat. "All I caught was my girl-friend sleeping with Sasquatch."

## THE END

# Honey Cummings

**A** passionate, award-winning author of Fantasy, Honey has turned her aim toward erotica. Blending everyday scenarios, and crafting them into steamy, blood-boiling moments for every shade of audience. Whether you want something short and hot, like a student-teacher hook up to the more paranormal flair, where Sleep with Sasquatch has unexpected bonus, look forward to erotic short stories, novellas, and hopefully a Trilogy in the future. Honey's debut erotic short landed at No. 3 in Urban Erotica and continues to satisfy readers time and time again. Be sure to leave her a review and let her know what you think!

amazon.com/Honey-Cummings/e/B07WFX5FDX
AuthorHoneyCummings.com
instagram.com/authorhoneycummings
twitter.com/HoneyCummings2
facebook.com/
Author-Honey-Cummings-101408818012749

# MORE BOOKS FROM 4 HORSEMEN PUBLICATIONS

## EROTICA

### ALI WHIPPE
Office Hours
Tutoring Center
Athletics
Extra Credit
Financial Aid
Bound for Release
Fetish Circuit
Now You See Me
Sexual Playground
Swingers
Discovered
XTC College Series Collection

### ARIA SKYLAR
Twisted Eros
Seducing Dionysus

### CHASTITY VELDT
Molly in Milwaukee
Irene in Indianapolis
Lydia in Louisville
Natasha in Nashville
Alyssa in Atlanta
Betty in Birmingham
Carrie on Campus
Jackie in Jacksonville
A Humorous Erotica Collection

### DALIA LANCE
My Home on Whore Island
Slumming It on Slut Street
Training of the Tramp
The Imperfect Perfection
Spring Break
72% Match
It Was Meant To Be... Or Whatever

### NICK SAVAGE
The Fairlane Incidents
The Fortunate Finn Fairlane
The Fragile Finn Fairlane
The Complete Package

# LGBT Erotica

### Dominic N. Ashen
Steel & Thunder
Storms & Sacrifice
Secrets & Spires
Arenas & Monsters
My Three Orc Dads: a Novella
Before the Storm: a Novella

### Eskay Kabba
Hidden Love
Not So Hidden
Signs of Affection
Deeply Devoted to Him
Honest Love
A Plane and Simple Connection

### Grayson Ace
How I Got Here
First Year Out of the Closet
You're Only a Top?
You're Only a Bottom?
I Think I'm a Serial Swiper
Lookin in All the Wrong Places
What Makes Me a Whore?
A Breach in Confidentiality
Back Door Pass
My European Adventure
An Unexpected Affair
Finding True Love
The Dr. Cage Chronicles

### Leo Sparx
Before Alexander
Claiming Alexander
Taming Alexander
Saving Alexander
The Fall of the House of Otter
The Case of Armando

### Robert Lewis
Someone to Love
Someone to Come Home To
Someone to Kiss

## Discover more at
## 4HorsemenPublications.com